Charren

P9-DHP-977

# SAFARI
# ADVENTURE

# SAFARI ADVENTURE

## Dick Houston

*With photographs by the author*

COBBLEHILL BOOKS

Dutton          New York

Copyright © 1991 by Dick Houston

*Library of Congress Cataloging-in-Publication Data*

Houston, Dick.
  Safari adventure / Dick Houston ; with photographs by the author.
    p.  cm.
  Includes index.
  Summary: Describes a safari in Kenya and Tanzania, highlighting
the native tribes, animals, and local scenery.
  ISBN 0-525-65051-2
  1. Kenya—Description and travel—1981-  —Juvenile literature.
2. Tanzania—Description and travel—1981-  —Juvenile literature.
3. Houston, Dick—Journeys—Africa, East—Juvenile literature.
[1. Kenya—Description and travel.  2. Tanzania—Description and
travel.  3. Safaris—Kenya.  4. Safaris—Tanzania.]  I. Title.
DT427.H67  1991

916.7604'04—dc20                 91-8038    CIP    AC

Published in the United States by Cobblehill Books,
an affiliate of Dutton Children's Books,
a division of Penguin Books USA Inc.

Printed in the United States of America
First Edition
10 9 8 7 6 5 4 3 2 1

For my mother and father, who taught me
to believe in making dreams come true.

For my sister, Emily Kaufman, who never let me
get discouraged, and then tirelessly deciphered
and transcribed my hopeless longhand scrawl
into several typewritten drafts. Thanks for being
a special person.

And thanks to my editor, who kept me on track
and made this book happen.

I got everyone lost on my first safari. While trekking with nine companions through entangled brush in thick woods, I lost sight of the trail. After an hour of hopelessly tramping in circles, crisscrossing our same tracks, my companions quickly lost their enthusiasm for adventure. Disaster had struck. It started to rain, my companions huddled together and started to cry. I had not had any previous experience as a "safari guide"—I was seven years old and in the first grade. Earlier on that eventful spring day at State Road School in Ashtabula, Ohio, during recess, I talked nine of my first grade classmates into going "on safari" into the gulf woods a mile from the school. Later, when I got everyone lost, I finally found the path and guided nine, drenched, bawling boys and girls—with torn trousers and dresses, and muddied little shoes—back to safety. When I got back home, my parents promptly grounded me, and my teacher banned me from recess for the rest of the year. I had unsuccessfully tried to recreate Stewart Granger's safari adventures in the "Dark Continent" after I had seen the film *King Solomon's Mines*. But I learned one important lesson early on—when things go wrong "on safari," keep your wits about you. Above all, keep your sense of humor.

My "safari fever" did not end in the first grade. As a youngster, through years of countless matinees at the local movie house, I saw every Technicolor African film Hollywood cranked out. As you will read in this book, it was the reruns of old black-and-white documentaries produced by the pioneer film makers Martin and Osa Johnson that fired my imagination. It was the Johnsons' behind-the-scenes look at how safaris operate with self-contained trucks, boxes and boxes of food, tents, camplife equipment, and enough spare parts to practically reassemble a vehicle that so fascinated me. By being able to set up camp in the middle of nowhere with everything they needed, even luxuries, the Johnsons had unlimited time to get to know the country, the African tribes, and the wild animals.

In my teens, I discovered the next best thing to studying the workings of an expedition life in the flesh was on circus lots of the many tent shows that frequented my hometown. For me, the real excitement began right after the night performance when the crowds dispersed, and the circus began to fold up its operations. Generators hummed with blazing eerie lights that flooded the circus lot on an Ohio hayfield, tents quickly sagged as twenty or so grumbling elephants pulled down the big-top poles, uprooted tent stakes, and then dragged huge rolls of canvas across the lot to the shouting commands of circus roustabouts. Within hours, the canvas city had been dismantled, rolled up, boxed up, and every item from mess tent equipment to circus hardware was neatly packed away into every nook and cranny of trucks. I always hung around until the last truck pulled off the lot. On one unforgettable night, I stood in the shadows next to the lion cage wagon parked off in a field. The pungent, musky odor of eight pacing lions in their cages was overpowering. Suddenly one of the lions stopped pacing and started to roar, at first with rhythmic grunts which set off the other seven lions. They stretched their necks and heads forward, their chests began heaving like giant bellows, working up to a feverish pitch of deafening roars that boomed with a paralyzing effect. They took no notice of me. Their eyes were intent on something far beyond the fields. What were they calling? A half-remembered dream of freedom on an African plain they had never seen? Why did I feel the pull too? At that moment, I knew I would never be the same again.

Some fifteen years later, I found myself listening to the roars of wild and free lions on the African plains, close to my tent. A dream of operating my own safaris had come true. When I first arrived in East Africa some twenty years ago, I had no delusions I was going to reinvent the safari. But in the early 1970s, big tour operators had turned safaris into mere sightseeing excursions—without the adventure. As you will read, I worked out an old formula based on the old adventure films I had seen as a kid. I never expected that often the greatest adventures would be the extraordinary people from ordinary backgrounds who signed up for my safaris because they wanted something challenging. It was the toss of the dice, since we did not seek the security of fancy lodges, nor did we carry guns. Those large, moving shadows just beyond the campfire light added an extra ounce of adrenaline.

There were always surprises off the beaten track, and the unexpected in camp—often with amusing results when things went wrong. Many clients discovered things about themselves on safari they did not know existed. Some seemed to be searching for something in their lives, and what they found was often greater than they expected. I, too, had a secret thing or place to search for. It was an old childhood image of a magic forested land, tucked away in a remote corner of Africa where Martin and Osa Johnson built a home in the 1920s, situated on the rim of a crater lake. The place was surrounded by more elephants than they could count. They called their home Lake Paradise. I wondered what was so magical about their secret lake, and if it still looked the same. I had to go there to find out.

Twenty years ago when I began running bush safaris, East Africa was a different world from what it is now. It was a far gentler place. There were still wonderful areas not overrun by tourists, especially in Kenya's Northern Frontier. There were fewer fences, fewer people, and more dirt roads, and certainly more wild animals. Today, it is a drastically different picture. Kenya's current population of 22 million people has one of the highest population growth rates in the world. The demands of its farmers, herders, and woodsmen for more land and timber are creating serious habitat problems for the country's wildlife. Poaching during the late 1970s and '80s was rampant, driving the rhino to near extinction. Today, newspapers and television worldwide headline the holocaust of the elephant all over Africa because of the illicit bloody ivory trade. In only ten years, Africa's elephant population has shrunk to less than 550,000 on the entire continent. But there is hope. In October of 1989, one hundred nations belonging to the Convention on International Trade in Endangered Species (CITES) voted to end all ivory imports and exports. Even though sixty nations refused to join the ivory ban, there has been a significant drop in ivory prices, and poaching is on the decline in Kenya and Tanzania. Being an optimist, I believe the tide can be turned if there are enough concerned people out there wanting to take an active role in conservation.

Perhaps in some small way, this book reveals nothing more than the simple joys of life—and why all this African magnificence must be saved for future generations. This is a story of one special safari, made up of one-of-a-kind individuals who came to Africa with little more in their pockets than a sense of fun, wild abandon, and a spirit of "anything is possible." They came because they felt they belonged—in the days before "adventure-travel" became trendy, safari chic in glossy tourist brochures.

My bush safari companions and I, for a time, lived a Huck Finn lifestyle. No one missed shopping malls, fast food stands, or television. It was almost as if Huck himself were around to say: "Enough of this civilizing nonsense. Let's go on safari!"

—Dick Houston
Lusaka, Zambia

# SAFARI ADVENTURE

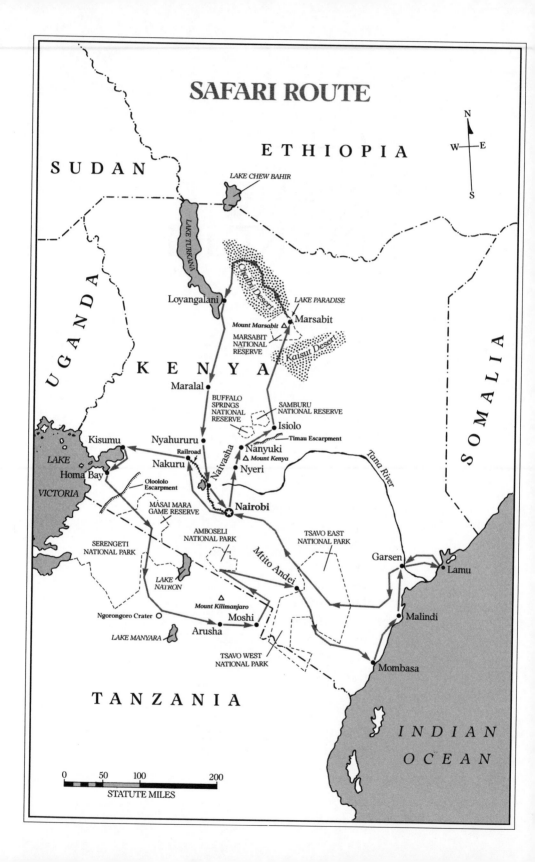

# 1

Bᴇᴛᴛᴇʀ ꜱᴇᴛ ᴜᴘ ʏᴏᴜʀ ᴏᴡɴ ᴛᴇɴᴛ ɴᴏᴡ," warned Jack as his flashlight winked off inside his tent. "The lions are a lot hungrier up here in the Northern Frontier." Out in the pitch blackness, I was relaxing in my canvas chair in the sand several yards distant from the tents of my traveling companions. I could just barely hear the faint "harumphing" calls of lions carried on the strong, warm night winds that thrashed the thorn trees all along the dry riverbed. The stars had perforated the blackness, transforming the night into a planetarium as a shooting star rocketed down to the horizon.

For the last several days I had been rattling over Kenya's vast semiarid Northern Frontier country with my safari partner, Jack, and five other companions. In 115-degree melting temperatures, we had pushed, pulled, coaxed, and bullied our two large safari vehicles—a grossly overloaded Land Rover and a supply van—through mud, sand, talcum powder dust, and then over black pumice rocks strewn about the volcanic desert landscape like thousands of discarded bowling balls. Endless maddening tire punctures, a bent drive shaft, and a boiling radiator contributed to the overheating of tempers. This is the "working part" of operating old-style bush safari adventures.

When the sun had begun to crouch behind the hills, we set up camp in the sandy dry riverbed. My companions and I had been too knocked out by the heat to prepare a campfire and hot meal; lukewarm canned beans turned out to be surprisingly delicious. When my friends practically crawled back to their tents to sleep, I was glad to have a few moments alone. A restorative drink loosened the cords of fatigue and aching muscles. The grunting of the lions became fainter and fainter until only the wind prowled across the black, baked landscape.

I was glad that these lions had moved off because the maneless desert lions (*Felis somaliense*) of the Northern Frontier—often traveling in pairs—are a bit more cunning than the lazy lion prides of the national parks where wild prey is plentiful for the taking. Survival on this parched land has made the desert lions relentless in pursuit of their quarry. It was a chilling thought that these nocturnal hunters could suddenly materialize before you in camp, having made no more noise than a spider walking up a mirror.

I marveled at the young shepherd boys of the pastoralist and seminomadic tribes, armed only with their spears, whose duty it is to watch over the goat flocks and cattle herds during the day. There have been many incidences when young boys have been brutally attacked, or carried off and eaten by desert lions. The Northern Frontier is not Tourist Africa.

In contrast to Kenya's shepherd boys, I thought back many years to when I was a kid, and my "encounter" with lions and Africa was under quite tame circumstances—at the movies. Back in the 1950s, I was invariably first in line at the Bula Theater in my hometown of Ashtabula, Ohio, to see *King Solomon's Mines, The African Queen, Mogambo,* and an endless stream of lush Technicolor safari films. But one particular type of movie had the most influence on me: a series of creaky black-and-white documentaries about Africa that had been produced decades earlier in the 1920s and '30s by Martin and Osa Johnson, a daredevil husband-and-wife film-making team from Kansas. The titles of their movies— *Jungle Adventures, Baboona, Congorilla*—were corny, but the Johnson formula for adventure was irresistible: mount an

2

elaborate safari, improvise various situations as you go along, and film them on the spot.

It was the gritty authenticity of those old reruns that made them so appealing to me. There were always the unexpected dangers of the Johnsons working so close to wild animals. A leopard once crashed through Martin's camera blind and landed on his lap. When Martin provoked a herd of elephants into charging the camera one day, Osa stood there dutifully cranking away until the last possible moment. Then she picked up her rifle and brought the herd leader crashing to the ground only inches from the tripod. The Johnsons organized meticulously planned motorized expeditions with fleets of safari cars that carried boxes and boxes of food, tents, rifles, motion picture equipment, tables, chairs, and even an ice-cream machine. By being self-contained on the road, the Johnsons were able to travel long distances over an extended period of time—and to be in control of when and where *they* wanted to go.

One magical place where the Johnsons did most of their filming fired my imagination. It was a remote crater lake atop a 5,900-foot forested mountain surrounded by a desert where, unharmed for centuries, the wild animals lived in a virtual garden of Eden. It was called Mount Marsabit, and was located in Kenya's Northern Frontier, some 260 miles from the nearest supply depot. It was there that they built a village and a motion picture laboratory on the rim of the crater lake; they planned to film the wildlife for four years. The lake was filled with egrets, cranes, ducks, and butterflies that fluttered over the water. There were more elephants than the Johnsons could count wandering along an ancient tree-lined path and gathering at the shoreline. When Osa had first gazed upon the lake, she exclaimed: "It's a paradise, Martin!" And from that moment on, that's what she called it: Lake Paradise.

For me, these images spilled over into childhood camping adventures during summer vacations—adventures that became learning experiences. My school buddies and I often set up tents alongside the Ashtabula River that meandered through a wooded gulf. Although we camped on the edge of town, on clear summer nights I imagined I was encamped on Mount Marsabit. I was charmed with the fact that the moon which glowed over the river was the very same moon which only hours earlier, and half a world away, had lighted the way for elephants on an old path at Lake Paradise. All those movies and summer camping "expeditions" gave me a dream: I was determined that some day I was going to operate my *own* adventure safaris in Africa.

There were times when I had my doubts that such a wild dream might be within reach for a Midwestern middle-class kid whose parents lived on a modest budget. It was an awfully long way from Ashtabula to Africa. Fortunately, I had parents who believed that life is what you make it. Even if you flop flat on your face at times, get right back up on your feet, and never quit on a dream. My father was an unpretentious, hardworking man who never tried to tame my free spirit. My mother believed that human worth was not measured by one's job, or bank account; dignity is worn on the inside. Special dreams have to be built on solid foundations.

This encouragement eventually led me to college where I received teaching degrees in English and history. When I started to teach junior high school in the mid-1960s, I was to discover that the teacher often learns just as much from his students. When I assigned several books on Africa—Ernest Hemingway's and Robert Ruark's safari stories, or Isak Dinesen's *Out of Africa* that chronicled the frontier days in British East Africa—the students' enthusiasm and fresh insights into these books made these stories come alive. The old African dream was rekindled into leaping flames.

The kids were always most excited about the safari way of life itself in the pioneer days. It was the singular appeal of those frontier days of a gypsy life on the road, free, setting up tents when and where some adventurer wanted to be. The word pictures of Africa in these old books focused on the mystique of Africa, a place where one could breathe. Everything was larger than life back then, and the African sky at night was like a slowly revolving dome, where the stars came down to your feet. It was as though your senses which you always took for granted were suddenly, by some grace, restored to you in Africa. You were whole again—you felt the pull of nature by being part of it.

One of the most popular books in the classroom was *Born Free*, the best-selling animal story of the 1960s, which told the true account of a Kenya game warden named George Adamson and his wife, Joy, who returned a tame lioness called Elsa back to the Kenyan bush. Joy Adamson also wrote *Living Free* and *Forever Free*, and her books alerted the world that Africa's wild places were disappearing almost overnight. My students were deeply disturbed by this fact, and did reports on Africa's human population explosion, rampant poaching of wildlife to supply the booming international trade in animal skins and ivory, and the alarming loss of wild habitats because of ever-growing agricultural and ranching schemes.

To illustrate what treasures of nature mankind would be losing, I read passages from Osa Johnson's *Four Years in Paradise* where she described a time when, decades ago, Africa was still an Eden frozen in time. One part of the book enchanted the students. Osa told of the time when the Johnsons left their Lake Paradise home for the last time. The year was 1927. Osa looked out over the lovely lake and said a little prayer, asking the Almighty to protect the place forever as a sanctuary for wildlife. The Johnsons died many years ago, and I wondered whether anything of that mystique of the "old Africa" might still remain intact.

Then, one day it happened, during one of those class discussions. A student hit me right between the eyes with a blunt question: "Hey, if you are so in love with Africa in books and films, why don't you stop talking about it and start doing something about getting there?" Other students picked up on this and excitedly talked about the possibilities of my searching for all those magical places we read about—before they faded away forever. Well, what was I waiting for? they urged.

The kids had me cornered there. Put your money where your mouth is. And leave it to kids to remind you that nothing ever happens in life unless you are willing to take a chance. It was then I decided to go to Africa to see it for myself. Somehow, I was going to find a way to operate my own safaris.

I had certainly had a lifetime of preparing myself for African travel in books, and I had learned where all the special places were by heart. But nothing takes the place of hands-on experience. Because I did not have this safari experience firsthand, I began to pore over many safari company brochures. I concluded that modern-day safaris had become big business—and, consequently, commercialized.

I went to several travel agents who connected me with people who had been on commercial safaris. I wanted to hear what their opinions were of such tours. Their conclusions were the same: large tour groups were packed into zebra-striped tour minibuses which traveled in tandem to expensive lodges. Although the lodges and hotels on these tours were lavish, there was no real feeling of being in a wild Africa. With only sixteen days or so of land travel, tour companies had milk-run itineraries that were packaged and predictable—never allowing for spontaneity to visit villages to meet the African people. Each morning, operating on a tight schedule, large groups at the lodges were herded into the buses merely to look at scenery and take snapshots of animals. In the afternoon, there was too much leisure time lolling about lodge swimming pools. At night, the safari program always dished out the same recipe when lodges put on "shows" for the tourists. Floodlights were turned onto man-made watering holes and salt licks which attracted the animals, but the blinding spotlights blotted out the African night and the stars. To the more adventurous travelers, these tours were too much like travelogues. Tourists were always seeing Africa from the same middle distance—either from a noisy lodge veranda, or through a bus window. I was convinced that this type of commercialized safari was far too "frilly," crowded, contrived, and tame for my liking. I decided that I would venture off on my own once I reached Africa.

I planned to take off for Kenya in the summer of 1972. Before leaving, I studied even more old safari books that gave me an idea for a safari formula for operating bush adventures. "Safari" is the Swahili word for "journey." Commercial, modern-day safaris were anything but journeys; they were primarily picture postcard tours where clients were treated as mere passengers. I knew that if my safaris were to be different, my clients could not be treated as passive observers.

There was one thread that ran through all those old Johnson books and movies—the Johnsons had been *participants* in adventures. Therein lay the key element to create my safari formula: Why not make my clients participants in the safari life itself? Each client should be treated as an individual—a fellow adventurer on a journey. My safari group would not be larger than six clients. The *modus operandi* would be to make safari vehicles self-contained with all the necessary supplies, permitting these journeys to venture off the beaten track for a month at a time, just as in the old days.

To do this, I had a plan in which my clients would be involved in every step of the safari lifestyle: help with safari preparations, help organize supplies, shop for food in the local and city markets, set up their own tents, even do their own laundry by the rivers, build campfires—and literally help push the vehicles over the rough spots in the bush. By being self-sufficient on the road, we would have the time and space for spontaneity. The more I thought of these possibilities, the more excited I got.

The spice of the journeys would be the anticipation of the unexpected: What new adventures would lie around the next bend in the track? What would happen when, while on foot outside a campsite, you come face to face with a six-ton bull elephant? What happens when a Cape buffalo trips over your tent ropes at night, or in the morning a troop of baboons sneaks into your campsite to steal from your food larders? What is it like to feel the ground shake beneath your feet as thousands of wildebeests in migration thunder in front of you? Unlike tours, real bush safaris should offer the adventure of the unknown.

Before I could develop this formula into a working system, I was going to need a safari partner—someone like myself who would be able to invest in a small safari business, needing a four-wheel-drive vehicle and all the equipment. Where could I find such an adventurous safari partner?

In an Africa guidebook, I happened across a tiny advertisement. It was for an old, English colonial-style, garden hotel, just at the edge of Nairobi, Kenya's capital city. It was called the Ainsworth Hotel, and it stressed that it was still a crossroads and meeting place for adventurers. I was going to check it out once I arrived in Nairobi.

After having scrimped on a teacher's salary for several years, I was ready to take off for Africa at the beginning of the summer of 1972. I had resigned from my teaching position, and in June I had my ticket in hand. I had done all my homework for the bush safari formula, and soon I was to be put to the test.

# 2

THE BOEING 707 began making its final descent through a blinding, early morning fog toward Kenya's Nairobi Airport. The plane was dropping fast over Nairobi National Park, whose fenced-in boundaries are close to the airport. Through holes in the fog, I got my first glimpse of the green Athi Plains, now only a few hundred feet beneath the wing. As the wheels dropped from the plane's belly with a roar, dark clusters of wildebeest and zebra herds were faintly visible below.

After landing, and then checking through customs, I found a taxi to take me to the Ainsworth Hotel at the edge of town. Only twenty minutes later, the taxi whisked under a tunnel of blue gum trees that lined Uhuru (Swahili for *freedom*) Highway. As the taxi sped along Uhuru, I was suddenly thrust into Nairobi's early morning, rush-hour traffic jams. Throughout the city, mini-skyscrapers, modern high-rise hotels, restaurants, supermarkets, boutiques, and large movie theaters reflected the revenues from Kenya's booming tourist trade. I noticed large crowds of tourists milling about hotel entrances, and I was glad I had chosen a hotel a little way from all the hubbub.

Although Nairobi looks much like any other modern, Western-style city, I was not prepared for the sudden appearance of a living relic from British East Africa's colonial days when my taxi pulled up in front of the Ainsworth Hotel. The hotel sits serenely on a hill above the city, situated much like a large English home on one- and two-story levels, set back from the road. When I left my taxi, and checked into the hotel, a friendly African receptionist led me to my room. I was a bit disoriented, though, when he opened a door. Expecting to see a closed-in hallway, I was suddenly out in the open, standing in an English garden, and looking up at fat white clouds sailing across azure Kenya skies. The hotel rooms are outside, set back along an open, sweeping veranda which surrounds the large, rectangular garden. Each room on the veranda faces a color riot of roses, gladiolas, cannas, cactuses, and a shower of purple bougainvillea draped over the rooms' red tin roofs. At one end of the courtyard, a neat little dining room, where tables were set with white linen and silverware, looks out onto a ten-foot-high poinsettia, jacaranda trees, frangipani, and the manicured lawn and hedges. When the African set my bags on the veranda outside my room, I felt I had found the perfect place. There was something wonderfully understated and peaceful about the Ainsworth—the place looked lived in.

The hotel is named after John Ainsworth, Nairobi's first Commissioner, who planted the city's blue gum trees that now proliferate in Nairobi. This hotel has stood here since 1910—a witness, for decades, to the changes from the pioneer days of British East Africa to the independent African nation of Kenya. At the turn of the century, frontier Nairobi was but a tiny refueling station (known as "Mile 326") on the Uganda Railway whose iron rails snaked upcountry from the Indian Ocean coast. In the early 1900s, Mile 326 faced rows of tin shacks perched on stilts above knee-deep mud. Zebras, giraffes, buffaloes, and antelopes stampeded down the streets; lions prowled the skirts of a swamp that was a noisy riot of chorusing frogs and humming mosquitoes. The town's first lodging, the Norfolk Hotel, built in 1904 (and just a mile downhill from the Ainsworth), was often "invaded" by roaring lions that snooped about the kitchen and dining room, sending staff and clientele sailing over tables, scrambling for cover. The Masai tribe that once lived near the swamp named this cold, 6,000-foot highland "Nyarobi," meaning "place of the cold waters." English pilgrims rode the then recently constructed railway up from Mombasa port toward the distant snow-capped Mount Kenya over the teeming zoological plains of British East Africa. They sought adventure at Mile 326—the halfway point on the railway between the coast and Lake Victoria. As I settled into the Ainsworth, I believed that those types of adventurous characters had become extinct.

In the days that followed my arrival, I soon found out that the Ainsworth was living up to its reputation as a crossroads. Each day, a few sojourners from all over the world—young men and women wearing backpacks—arrived at the hotel looking for people to share trip expenses. The Ainsworth seemed a ready-made place for the camper-type of clients I would need. But needing to find a safari partner came first, so I decided to hang around the hotel for a while longer. Two weeks later, and with no luck, I thought such prospects might be hopeless. Then, one afternoon, something happened which changed the picture completely.

I was sitting at a table in the cozy Ainsworth tavern, poring over Michelin East Africa maps spread across several tables. Absorbed, I focused on territory not trodden by tourists. Then, quite unexpectedly, a long shadow fell over my maps.

"What are you looking for in all those maps, Yank . . . treasure?" This voice shot out of a tall, lanky, young Britisher with thick sandy hair who was suddenly standing right over my table. Without asking, he pulled up a chair across from me, plunked his bony frame into it, and started to regale me with his great adventure.

He introduced himself as Jack Thornton, and announced he'd just arrived from England under rather unusual circumstances. Having quit his job as a car mechanic in London, he risked everything on a wild dream. He talked two of his buddies into embarking upon, of all things, an overland trip from England to East Africa. After rigging out a Land Rover

11

(an indestructible four-wheel-drive vehicle manufactured by British Leyland), they were off on a 10,000-mile journey across a rugged Africa. Their three-month safari took them across the scorching, 130-degree temperatures of the Sahara Desert, and then into remote bush country of central Africa. During heavy rains in Zaire (formerly the Congo), the Land Rover sunk up to its doors in a soupy morass of mud, the consistency of melted taffy. Facing the many gritty challenges of "roughing it" across Africa, they were initiated into the true safari way of life that permitted them to travel off the beaten track. When the trip ended at Nairobi, two of the Englishmen reluctantly had to take a plane back to their mundane, routine jobs in London.

"But I couldn't tear myself away," Jack said. "Enchantress Africa had wormed her way into my blood. Now, I've been toying with an idea of running camping safaris throughout Kenya and Tanzania. When I snooped around Nairobi, I discovered that even the *camping* safari companies are commercialized. Usually twenty-five passengers or so are packed onto the back of an open Bedford truck, and then hauled like cattle from one prearranged campsite to the next. I've been trying to come up with a different approach—and find areas far from tourist crowds." Jack stopped suddenly, looked hard at the maps for a moment, and then squinted at me: "Got any ideas, Yank?"

"Have I got any ideas?" I laughed. "Only a lifetime of them. I think my whole life leads up to this moment. Hang on a while and I'll tell you."

Before I knew it, I had talked over an hour about my own ideas for operating safaris. I spelled out the safari formula of restricting a safari party to six clients, and including them in on the action as a working team. It was an old formula, of course. In essence, I wanted to recreate the spirit of the bush adventures of yesteryear, journeying for one month at a time, to explore areas that still had the flavor of the Old Africa—before it was gone forever. I stressed that even though Jack lived under primitive conditions during his overland journey, a small safari business would have to attract clients by offering comforts—even a few luxuries. To carry the extra equipment and provisions, it would be necessary to buy an additional vehicle. By being self-contained with *two* vehicles, we could cover a wide expanse of East Africa.

I detailed a few magic places of bush country I had read about, such as the Northern Frontier. Jack perked up when I mentioned Martin and Osa Johnson and their adventures at Lake Paradise. It was now taking little persuasion to convince Jack. Straight off we had sensed what we had in common: a thirst for adventure and the willingness to take a chance.

"You need go no further," Jack interrupted. "You don't need to convert the converted. I think we just became safari partners. But this old safari formula is going to need some trial and error by operating several short safaris to get the hang of it, and check out those special places you mention. While doing short trips, we can learn firsthand some ideas for the logistics of running one-month safaris."

Jack stood up, and we shook hands to seal our safari partnership. He then led me outside to the Ainsworth's tree-shaded parking lot to check out his long-wheel-base Land Rover. Jack's resourcefulness of making much from little was evident. The Land Rover was made-to-order and could go anywhere over an extended period of time. Preparing for his overland trip, Jack had improvised by constructing an 80-gallon petrol tank on the Land Rover's roof. Additional petrol and water jerry cans were fastened onto the front and rear bumpers. A large, homemade roof rack held luggage, engine spare parts, camping equipment, wooden boxes for tinned food, shovels, steel cables with a winch for getting out of mud, and steel sand tracks for placing under tires when stuck in desert sands.

We discussed our overall plans for the one-month trips, and agreed that an additional vehicle would be indispensable.

13

In the days that followed, working out some initial details, we hunted around Nairobi and found a perfect vehicle for our safari workhorse: a large van with a wide, sliding door on the driver's side. We planned to convert this van into our supply wagon. We would later transfer some Land Rover equipment to the van to leave more seats for clients in both vehicles. To make money to cover our investment, we planned to run short safaris at intervals during the next several months. In between those safaris, and once back at the Ainsworth, we would whip the van into shape.

For the six-day or eight-day short runs, we could take only three clients in the Land Rover. Word soon got around the Ainsworth, and for the next several months, we never had any trouble filling the three seats. These short runs were an experiment to check out the best areas for camping. On each successive trip, we varied our routes. Some six- or eight-day runs traveled on the fringes of the Northern Frontier, or to western Kenya. Other short runs concentrated on the Kenya coast only—where we found many deserted beaches for camping. Some trips investigated Kenya's game country, while other short runs traveled straight to northern Tanzania to check out the less-trodden game country there. By the end of 1972, we planned to combine all these different routes into our one-month safari. We set the latter part of December for the inauguration of the grand safari.

In the time between the short-run safaris, we worked like demons rigging out the van in the Ainsworth's parking area. During those months, we hammered together shelves and cupboards inside the van. Each storage compartment was designed to organize various supplies for instant access on the road. Cabinets and wooden boxes were securely fastened to the van's walls and floorboards. They stored hardware such as spare wheels, tires, tire repair kits, crowbars, axes, shovels, a barbecue grate for campfire cooking, a monster-size tea kettle, army-size pans for washing dishes, and the necessary first-aid kit. We "invented" labor-saving devices for doing the laundry: two huge plastic buckets with seal-tight lids became our automatic washer and rinse cycle. The bumpy bush roads would make a sloshingly-good agitator.

We created a complete, working safari kitchen on wheels: just inside the van's sliding door, a large propane cooking stove swung out on hinges for convenience. (The stove would be necessary when a rain shower might douse the campfire.) A canvas tarp rolled out from above the van door for a canopy over our fresh air kitchen. A folding worktable slid up and out from the van floor. Inside, a large sliding-door cupboard held securely a large pressure cooker, pots and pans, kitchen utensils, and plates, cups, and glasses. (The silverware was wrapped tightly in newspaper to prevent it from rattling on the road like tin wind chimes in a cement mixer.) A long, collapsible dining table was stored neatly behind the van's back seat.

On those various six- and eight-day runs, we had learned that clients wanted baths after a jolting, hot, and dusty day on the road. We made a portable camp shower from a large canvas bucket with a shower head attached. A rope on a pulley would be slung over a high tree branch at camp to hoist the bucket above the ground. A clamp on a plastic hose regulated the flow of water from the bucket to the shower head. To add more conveniences, we purchased canvas folding chairs, extra tables, pressure lamps, washstands, cots, and a large electric lamp (operated on the Land Rover's battery) for a working light in the kitchen.

We decided that each client should have his or her own private tent. To save some labor and time at campsites, I purchased the newer-type tents which use a color-code system of easy assembly, interconnecting poles—thereby saving the pounding in of stakes and guy wires. The printed directions looked so simple that I did not bother to try setting up the new tents—a decision I would later regret.

We also had learned that clients had groaned about bland food from cans, so we decided to add a few "luxuries." We

15

would prepare elaborate meals that would be grilled steaks, pork chops, lamb, chicken dishes, fresh fruits, and vegetables—and even fresh seafood when camping on the Kenya coast. To preserve these perishable provisions while on the road, our "refrigerator" consisted of two large Coleman coolers which would be packed with Dry Ice purchased in Nairobi on the day of departure. (The meats would be frozen solid in the Ainsworth's deep freeze two days before leaving.) When the Dry Ice ran out, we'd have to use imagination to prepare tasty meals of rice dishes, pastas, spaghetti, some canned concoctions, or even try some African dishes. Jack was suspicious of my culinary ambitions when I used him as a guinea pig. The "great chef" prepared a creamed chicken dish at the Ainsworth. When I set the dish on the table, Jack gaped in horror; it was slimy, underdone, yet burnt on the edges. Jack pushed it around the plate with his fork, and curled his lip. "Yep, it's creamed chicken all right—a chicken that was just *creamed* on Uhuru Highway." The clients would have to take their chances.

For the grand safari, the clients would help us shop for fresh provisions at the African market in Nairobi.

By the end of November, after having completed many six-day runs, the Land Rover and van were ready for takeoff around the middle of December. Our itinerary would be open, but generally combining those areas from the separate short-run safaris. We purposely timed our inaugural one-month's journey to camp on the Serengeti Plain in Tanzania to coincide with the awesome migrations of hundreds of thousands of wildebeests, zebras, and antelopes in late December and early January.

Keeping to the spirit of spontaneity, we would vary our means of travel and areas of interest. We had decided on something different for the first leg of our grand safari. Since the Uganda Railway was so much a part of the old days in Kenya, we wanted our clients to experience a trip on an old steam train across the Rift Valley. This would have special meaning, since most of the old steam engines were rapidly being retired from service.

And instead of just looking at Mount Kilimanjaro, we planned a foot safari up to its snow-capped peak. On previous runs to the Kenya coast, we had visited an ancient Arab town on Lamu Island. Our clients would explore Lamu's old streets and alleyways—a place changed little in its 1,000-year-old history. No two days on this safari would be the same.

At the beginning of December, I began advertising at the Ainsworth. I discovered that the variety of our safari was a big drawing card, and soon I had several bites. Within days, four young men and women signed up for the journey.

Jack and I had learned that the rigors of bush travel were demanding and taxing. Because of this, we made a rule: we would not sign on anyone over fifty-five years of age. The rule was ironclad—and there would be no exceptions, no matter what.

As mid-December rolled around, Jack and I were satisfied with our work. Every detail, each item for supplies, had been checked over on lists a hundred times. All our plans and regulations seemed perfect . . . until one day something momentarily upset the apple cart.

Out of the blue, on a bright December morning at the Ainsworth, just two days before takeoff on the big safari, a sixty-eight-year-old, red-haired grandmother from Manhattan walked straight into the hotel—and into our lives. It was the start of a most unusual safari in which anything could happen.

# 3

On that memorable sunny december morning, the Ainsworth parking lot looked as though the circus had just come to town. Boxes and boxes of supplies, rolled-out tents, canvas tarps, and sundry other materials were set out on the gravel lot, completely surrounding the two safari vehicles.

Our four young safari clients, who were helping with some last minute inventories on the boxes in the lot, appeared to be the perfect traveling companions. Each one of them had had some experience with African travel. Brian Shipton and Pete Messener, two strapping American men in their twenties, had been hitchhiking for a few months in West and Central Africa. Aya Andersen and Ulla Scholl, two attractive women in their twenties, were nurses from Denmark, now employed in a small, upcountry hospital in western Kenya. These young people were enthusiastic and readily pitched in to help get the show on the road. The gals helped organize all tinned goods, rice, flour, sugar, and other bulk-packaged foods, while the guys lifted heavy materials into the van and onto the Land Rover's roof rack.

Earlier that morning we had bought the meat and put it in the Ainsworth's deep freeze. The next day we would purchase the vegetables and fruit in the City Market.

Since it was an exceptionally hot day in the lot, we decided to take a break at noon to cross-check our lists at tables in the Ainsworth's small patio area at the front of the hotel.

Jack and I had ordered ice-cold Cokes while Aya, Ulla, Brian, and Pete wrote down the perishable food items we would need at the City Market.

But then, suddenly, something caught my eye among all the potted plants, cactus, and bougainvillea. A large, pink "orange blossom," the size of a basketball, momentarily flashed between the gaps in the vegetation and then bobbed along the top of a hedge. Now my companions noticed, and we all leaned forward in our chairs, our Coke glasses paused in midair, fascinated as the "orange flower" appeared and then disappeared between the poinsettias, then bobbed toward the cactus whose long needles seemed to reach out trying to impale this animated "flower" for examination. The "blossom" left the greenery, found an opening in the garden, and took human form. The "blossom" belonged to a short, older woman with a Raggedy Ann mop of short, curly, orange-red hair.

The woman stopped in her tracks, looked quickly to the left, then to the right, almost mechanically. Then she opened her enormous shoulder bag that was slung over her red, blue, and green flower-pattern muu-muu, reached in and dug up a pack of cigarettes, lit up and took a few quick puffs. She walked forward with mincing steps like a little wren, leaned over a potted palm, and squinted into the patio area. She stood there with one hand on her hip, pushed back her out-sized blue-rimmed glasses on her nose, and ran her fingers nervously through her tousled hair. She was now staring intently at us. Then she walked straight up to our tables and asked, "Are you the fellas who operate adventure camping safaris?"

Before I could answer, she had spotted our safari gear and food larder lists and asked if she could pull up a chair to join us. Up close, I could see that she was at least in her late sixties; her muu-muu hung loosely on a slightly hunched-over, small frame. There was something instantly appealing about her. Her large brown eyes made her appear wistful, almost waiflike.

"I hope you don't mind my intrusion," she apologized, "but I just now saw your advertisement that was posted on the thorn tree bulletin board at the New Stanley Hotel's sidewalk cafe. I just arrived back in Africa from New York, and checked into the Ainsworth in the wee hours this morning. But I was too excited to sleep, so I stayed up until dawn and then walked into town. I've been looking about for some type of camping safari. Your trips look like the adventure I've been searching for."

Jack and I did need to fill another seat or two, but Jack cast a "warning shot" frown at me. He would not budge on the cutoff rule at age fifty-five. When Pete asked her what brought her to Africa, "Orange Blossom" spoke up: "I was here in Kenya two years ago for a few weeks on a package, tour-group safari, and I fell in love with the country. I met some lovely people on the tour, but I found that they whined too readily about the heat and the dust. Of course, there were the few, wearisome *nouveau riche* tourists who spent most of their energies bragging about their importance back home, and they worked hard at ignoring me. I often ended up eating by myself at the lodges. But I think I saw an Africa they didn't see. I had my best time, though, after the tour ended and I decided to travel around the country on my own for a couple of weeks. I discovered that when I really touched the country, the African people opened up and welcomed me. I found that side of Africa to be the place where I could be myself." Suddenly, she stopped talking for a moment. "Oh, I'm afraid I might be boring you."

"Far from it, please go on," Aya piped up, intrigued with this woman.

"Well," she continued a little nervously, "it was a lifetime dream to come to Africa someday, but I grew up in the Depression and such a wild idea of going to Africa was way out of the question. Only books and movies kept the dream alive. Two years ago, my three sons and their wives gave me a surprise present: a ticket to Africa. I was flabbergasted.

20

When I got to Kenya, I found it more beautiful than I had imagined. After I got back to New Jersey, I knew I had to get back to Africa to stay. But my husband died many years ago, I had little money, and I felt I might be too old for such things anyway. Then last year while working at my job as a secretary in a Manhattan office, someone tacked a poster over my desk that read: 'This is the first day of the rest of your life.' So I thought about that for awhile, and said to myself, 'Elaine, you've always had to learn to do things on your own, and you're not getting any younger.' I felt like those birds on the Galapagos Islands that, even though they had wings, they'd forgotten how to fly. So, soon afterwards, I quit my job. Then I sold my little house in Jersey, had a giant garage sale, sold off all my possessions, and cried for days after I had said my good-byes to my grandchildren. My sons had a fit, of course, believing I had taken leave of my senses. But the important thing now is that I am *here*!"

Her disarming manner and enthusiasm I could see were bringing the faintest smile to the lips of "Old Skeptic" Jack. Somehow I could not imagine a grandmother surviving a one-month safari that required so much stamina. Jack and I made a fatal error in trying to throw her off the track by stressing the physical demands of our itinerary.

"I should caution you," Jack started off, trying to let her down easy. "My companions here are taking off two days from now on the morning train to Kisumu at Lake Victoria. An African driver and I will drive the vehicles to meet them at Homa Bay on the lake. That's the easy part. We're all packed and ready to go. We don't take anyone over fifty-five years of age because the *rest* of the journey will be exhausting. We'll be climbing Kilimanjaro, snorkeling on the coast, digging the vehicles out of the sand and mud in the Northern Frontier, changing flat tires surrounded by wild animals. To say nothing of sitting in a nomads' encampment and chewing leathery goat meat and . . ."

"Well, please excuse me for interrupting," Orange Blossom

spoke up, "but first off, my stuff is still packed in several suitcases. Can I adapt to difficult situations? I've dug my old Chevy out of four-foot-deep snowdrifts, changed bald tires on the New Jersey turnpike during rush hours. If you can survive that, you can survive anything. And chewing goat meat? Look, this hair may be a tad dyed these days, but I still have my *own* teeth. I can do anything—except climb mountains."

I could see Aya and Ulla trying to keep straight faces as they watched the "steely safari men" trying to worm their way out of this one.

"And who do you suppose," Elaine persuaded, "is going to have all your comforts ready at the end of an exhausting day? You don't want boring meals from cans when you're really hungry, do you? I'm the best gourmet cook around. I stole every recipe I could get my hands on in New York restaurants. And I make a mean spaghetti."

Jack and I were losing this verbal fencing match, and gradually we watched our once ironclad rule of "No one over fifty-five" turn to mush.

"Okay! Okay!" Jack threw up his hands in surrender. "I hope you know this is all highly irregular. You are now officially appointed the Safari's Chief Cook and Bottle Washer. But I warn you—if your spaghetti and the gastronomic delights you boast of don't live up to snuff, we throw you to the lions!"

Elaine puffed triumphantly on her cigarette. "Well, fine with me. It will beat dying in an Old Folks' home."

Jack then cautioned Elaine of one strict rule which applied to all passengers: "Do not bring all of your suitcases. Pack one small bag only. And tomorrow I'll put you to work picking out the best vegetables at the City Market. You'll find the African market quite an adventure."

As we got up to leave the tables, we all agreed to meet at the hotel entrance early the next morning to go to the City

Market. Elaine stopped me for a second to ask me one more question: "Do you carry guns on your safaris?"

"No," I answered, "but just in case anyone is attacked by lions, I carry a bugle for 'Taps.' "

Elaine's eyes flooded with tears and she began rummaging through her shoulder bag. "I always need lots of Kleenex when I laugh," she said, dabbing at her eyes.

The following morning we drove the Land Rover and van into Nairobi for last-minute errands. Our first stop was the City Market, and any comparison to a modern supermarket ends as soon as you enter the place. Housed within a huge, cavernous cement barn, the African market vibrates with more action than a free beer day in a Wild West saloon. Inside, you are instantly overwhelmed by the mishmash of smells of fresh vegetables and fruit of all description. Row upon row of hawkers' stalls are heaped high with towering mountain ranges of produce: huge heads of lettuce and cabbages, bursting tomatoes, giant avocados, juicy pineapples, mangoes, limes, and stalks of bananas that threaten to let loose an avalanche. Brian, Pete, Aya, and Ulla never ceased to marvel at the sheer size of Kenya vegetables. "I think these mushrooms here," Elaine exclaimed, "have a thyroid condition." Some mushrooms were the size of baseballs.

Other counters filled with ice were heaped with pink shrimp, lobster, and giant crab which are shipped fresh daily from the Kenya coast.

Since Jack and I always did a volume of business here, the hawkers knew us on sight and converged on us like hungry lions. "Come with me, Bwana!" they all jabbered, surrounding us, grabbing hold of our arms, practically carrying us off to their stalls. We were all laughing at their hard-sell haggling tactics that put Wall Street to shame. They try for the highest price until you pretend indifference and try to walk away saying, "Too expensive." But the hawkers come stampeding after you, and instantly lower their prices. Once the price is agreed upon, African boys begin filling your boxes and baskets to overflowing, and then hoist them onto their heads to carry them to your vehicles. It is all good-natured fun that takes place every day of the year, since Kenya has a year-around growing season.

Later that day we picked up the Dry Ice, got petrol, and finished other errands. When we got back to the Ainsworth, we were worn out. But we were excited about getting up early the next day to be at Nairobi station to catch the morning train to Lake Victoria in western Kenya. A friend, Margaret Chamberlin, who was a Peace Corps volunteer at Homa Bay on the lake, would board us for the night at her home as we waited for Jack and the African driver to arrive with the vehicles the following day.

During dinner in the Ainsworth's little dining room, Jack reminded "Orange Blossom" to travel light. "Remember," he stressed, "pack only one small bag. No other luggage."

Elaine blinked innocently through her glasses and smiled. "Yes, I understand," she said. "Bring only one bag."

Promptly at 6:30 the next morning, that great English tradition of early morning tea was brought silently to my hotel room by an old *mzee* (a Swahili term for an older man). He tapped gently on the door. "*Chai*, Bwana." The warming cup of tea helped wake up a groggy head. I had slept fitfully because I was excited about one special aspect of our journey; we'd be making our first visit ever to Lake Paradise.

After finishing my tea, I hurried to the breakfast table where I found Aya, Ulla, Brian, and Pete sitting together. Their small carry-on-size bags were packed neatly beside them. But there was no sign of Elaine.

"Where is Orange Blossom . . . er, I mean, Elaine?" I asked, a little concerned. My companions believed that she was still in her room organizing her bag.

We had to get a move on since the two taxis were already

waiting at the hotel entrance to take us down to the train station. I ran down the open veranda to Elaine's room, and found her door wide open. Elaine greeted me cheerily, dressed in a fresh blue-flowered muu-muu, her orange hair slightly damp from the shower. I had just started to ask her where her bag was when out of the corner of my eye, I thought I saw a human corpse stretched out full-length on the bed. But it wasn't a body, it was the longest, fattest, lumpiest canvas duffel bag I had ever seen in my life! Clothes and indescribable objects were peeking out of the draw string at the top of the green bag. The thing must have weighed 150 pounds. In disbelief, I said, "I think you must have stuffed your old Chevy in there."

Elaine looked a little sheepish and said, "Well, you *did* say only one bag."

With mounting irritation, I stammered a bit, incredulous at the sheer size and length of that bag. "You see," she nervously added, "I just couldn't bear to part with my toiletries, extra muu-muu's, shorts, swimsuits, and a few other necessities like my tape player and all my Johnny Mathis tapes and . . ."

I stopped her in mid-inventory and told her there was no time to repack now since we might miss the train. Then, hurriedly, Elaine and I got at each end of the bag, gripping a hold like two grave robbers removing a corpse. The dead-weight bag slumped in the middle and swung back and forth as our two bent-over figures tried to navigate it through the door. It got stuck in the door jamb, and we lost our grip. We tried again and dropped it again. I was beginning to do a slow burn as my fingers went numb.

We finally stuffed it through the door. We hunched over again, like gnomes, trying to grip the canvas bag that seemed as spineless as a giant sea slug. We shuffled along the veranda as hotel guests in the dining room stared at us through the windows. We suddenly glanced at each other, realizing how ridiculous we looked, and then collapsed to the floor, reduced to quaking heaps of hysterical laughter. Elaine tried to pass me a Kleenex.

Once we regained some composure, we dragged the bag to the hotel front. Aya, Ulla, Brian, and Pete were standing there. Their jaws dropped open when they saw us coming down the corridor. The two taxi drivers practically shrieked: "Eeeeee! Bwana! This is very bad. We'll never get that thing into the taxi." But when I slipped them some extra shillings, the Africans manhandled The Bag into one of the car trunks, where it dropped in with a thud.

"You're just darn lucky Jack hasn't seen this!" I said. "He'd ban you from the trip on the spot." Just then, Jack was walking over from the parking lot where he and the African driver were getting the vehicles ready to take them to Homa Bay the following day.

After saying our good-byes to Jack, we piled into the two taxis and took off through Nairobi's morning rush hour traffic to the train terminal.

# 4

As SOON AS WE REACHED THE STATION, we saw the long passenger train with its cream-and-maroon coaches being boarded by hundreds of Africans. Nothing gets the blood stirring faster than the puffing of an old steam engine, the smell of its acrid smoke and iron. To me, the steam train is the most romantic assemblage of iron and steel ever devised by man.

After we purchased our tickets, and two porters grumbled about carrying Elaine's bag, we walked out onto the platform. Watching all the action, it took little imagination to conjure up images of pioneer days when English settlers and safari hunters, caked in red dust, disembarked at Station 326 from the Uganda Railway, which the Africans called the Iron Snake. In those colonial days, a long line of rickshaw taxis waited at the station's front to transport weary travelers over Nairobi's dusty streets to the Norfolk Hotel.

We were soon moving through a throng of Africans who appeared to be carrying everything they owned in dilapidated cardboard boxes tied up with ropes. The most engaging thing about Africans is their openness, saying good-byes with bone-crushing hugs, a mixture of tears, and loud laughter.

All along the coaches, African men and women were clustered at the open windows, leaning halfway out with outstretched arms to receive gifts of maize, fruit and vegetable baskets, and even live chickens from family and friends. Once we boarded the train and squeezed our way down the narrow coach passageways, we were greeted by many friendly Africans with a hearty "Jambo!"—the Swahili word for "hello." There is nothing comparable to "Jambo" in any other language. "Jambo" is a salute, a handshake, a greeting of the spirit.

After the porters placed our bags in our respective berths, we all headed for the dining car. A few shrill, teakettle-like whistle blasts announced "All Aboard," and the engine tugged at its coaches and pulled us out of the station. We clacked slowly along through the quiet suburbs of Nairobi, passing by many English-style, quarry-stone cottages and a large golf course. Once we took our seats in the dining car, I pointed out to my companions the undulating ridge of the green velvet Ngong Hills in the distance. The Ngong Hills were immortalized by the Danish writer, Karen Blixen, who in colonial times owned a large coffee plantation near the Ngong. Karen Blixen, under the pen name Isak Dinesen, wrote the classic *Out of Africa.*

Thirty miles outside of Nairobi, the earth suddenly dropped out from under us: we had approached the dizzying edge of the Great Rift Valley. Two thousand feet or so below us was a great thorn bush landscape, punctuated by the dramatic rise of Mount Longonot crater cone in the distance. As the train skirted the Rift's edge, we could see some forty miles across the valley to the other side of the escarpment wall where clouds lined the edge. Thousands of years ago a fault in the earth created the Rift, some fifty miles wide in places, that gouges its way from lower Russia, down across Africa to what is now Zimbabwe in southern Africa. The Rift is so large that American astronauts could see it in its entirety after they had landed on the moon.

The engine's brakes screeched, preparing for the descent into the Valley. The puffing engine continually came into full side view as the coaches twisted and swayed, zigzagging along the gentler grade. The Rift's floor seemed to move farther away the closer we approached, the train shrinking in size as the escarpment wall loomed behind us.

As the train stretched out onto the Valley floor and entered thorn bush country, we saw several giraffes and zebras right smack in the middle of a large herd of cattle. More and more of the open country is being taken over by herders for goats, sheep, and cattle. Wild animals must now compete for the best grazing land with domestic stock.

The floor of the Rift became steeper as we climbed to a higher elevation and eventually passed Lake Naivasha and Lake Elementeita. It was in this area that many English settlers set up large ranches and farms. In the early 1900s, Lord Delamere, Kenya's legendary pioneer settler, started up the colony's first wheat farms and cattle ranches near Elementeita. Delamere was largely responsible for encouraging English settlement and for laying the foundations of an agricultural economy in Kenya.

An hour or so later, the engine belched sparks and black smoke as we continued to climb toward a cluster of red-roofed houses and buildings of Nakuru town, which rests on a high hill. At the foot of this town lies a large lake. We would disembark at Nakuru station, and later catch the midnight train to Kisumu on Lake Victoria. At Lake Nakuru, we would witness one of the greatest phenomena of nature in the world. It was Elaine who first spotted something strange about the lake which was now spread out below us to our left as the train approached the station.

"The shores of that lake are pink," she said, puzzled. "And that lake shore seems to be *moving*."

I stood up and craned my neck out the open window. "Your eyes are not deceiving you," I said. "You are looking at a pink lake all right—made up of over two million flamingos."

Aya and Ulla, who had visited the lake before, told Elaine, Brian, and Pete to be prepared to see the greatest bird spectacle on earth.

Soon after we pulled into Nakuru station and disembarked

from the train, we left our bags with the station master and hired two taxis to take us into town. Although it was December and the beginning of the dry season, the Nakuru area was still experiencing the tail end of late afternoon showers. Large black clouds were beginning to hang low over the town.

After a late lunch at the old Stag's Head Hotel, we were driven off in our taxis for the shores of the lake. Passing through the gates of Nakuru National Park, a sudden cloudburst bolted across the heavens, drenching our hopes of seeing the flamingos. The rain pelted down on the muddy road in a steady flood.

But as quickly as it had started, the rain suddenly stopped at 5:30 P.M. We had just over an hour of daylight left, and cloudy and dull at that. (Near the equator, darkness arrives around 7:00 P.M.) Driving farther along the road, trees at first blocked our view. They eventually thinned out and disappeared, and we got a sweeping view of the lake. The sun suddenly found an opening in the blackened sky and cast its beams onto the water. The effect was startling. A giant black backdrop was lowered from the sky, the floodlights of sun switched onto a shimmering lake of pink. The stage had been set, and the flamingos were the main attraction. As we drove closer to the lake, we could barely believe the spectacle before us. No matter how many times you may see this, you are never prepared for the emotional impact.

The lake was now a virtual sea of living pink. We stepped out of the cars and walked toward the shore. A chilling wind was blowing with great strength from across the water, carrying with it the deafening voices of over two million birds. There was no other sound but these "voices," and the flapping of millions of wings—a pink forest of phosphorescent feathers constantly vacillating, rising, falling, and shifting like trillions of sequins blowing in the wind.

It is nearly impossible to comprehend that so many birds could gather in one place at one time. It is the algae and minute crustaceans that live in Nakuru's soda waters which attract the flamingos in such overwhelming numbers. Two species of flamingo are found here: the lesser flamingo which feeds on the algae, and the greater flamingo that feeds on the brine shrimp and other crustaceans.

We were all deeply moved by the majesty of such a scene. Before we knew it, darkness was beginning to descend over the lake, and we reluctantly got back in the cars and returned to the town. We stopped off at the Stag's Head for supper and talked on into the evening, sharing our impressions of the flamingos. We snapped to attention when we heard the distant whistle of the night train approaching Nakuru, and ran out into the night to catch our waiting taxis that would rush us to the terminal. Just as we picked up our bags, the train came pounding into the station, streams of light from the coach windows gliding along the platform. With no time to spare, we scrambled aboard our coach and got to our respective berths. Soon after the train pulled out of Nakuru, I fell fast asleep, rocking and swaying as the coaches clacked along the fringes of a black, cold forest.

Early the next morning when the sun shot through the windows of the dining car, Aya and Ulla caught the first glimpse of an enormous blue patch of water far below the Valley at the foot of green rolling hills. It was Winam Gulf of Lake Victoria. The train continued to descend through cotton balls of mist hovering over patches of cultivated fields. We were now feeling the sticky humidity of the lake, and the cold air of the highlands was but a memory.

Dropping more in elevation, we caught sight of the wider expanse of Lake Victoria, the second largest freshwater lake in the world after Lake Superior. Lake Victoria is one of the most fabled bodies of water in history; it is the source of the Nile River. For many centuries the source of the Nile had remained an unsolvable mystery to the ancient Egyptians whose civilization sprang from the Nile. It wasn't until 1858 that British explorer John Henning Speke, on an overland expedition, found the great lake. It was later confirmed that this body of water was indeed the Nile's source. Speke named the lake after Queen Victoria.

We were just finishing breakfast as the train puffed through the outskirts of Kisumu near the lake. Gradually we came to a grinding halt in the station. I felt a bit sentimental knowing that all steam trains in Kenya would soon be replaced by diesel engines. To me, a diesel is but a functionary machine totally devoid of personality.

The station was now alive with activity as African men and women began passing their boxes, baskets, and even babies through the windows to the waiting arms of families and friends. A hectic scene was also unfolding inside our own coach passageway. Elaine was trying to convince two balky African porters that her duffel bag was lighter than it looked. A few extra shillings did the trick, and the groaning porters hoisted the bag between them onto their shoulders and staggered off the train.

As we disembarked from the train into the crowd, I was hoping that my friend Margaret Chamberlin would be waiting for us at the station. We would be staying the night at Homa Bay where she worked as a Peace Corps volunteer with the Luo tribe.

Having been to Homa Bay before, I was secretly smiling to myself since I knew our transport there would be a hair-raising experience for my unsuspecting companions.

Having navigated through the crowd to the taxi stand, I recognized an elegant, middle-aged American woman in khaki slacks, shirt, and red bandana, waving her arms above the crowd to get our attention. Margaret Chamberlin rushed up to us and, after quick introductions, she told us she had two taxis waiting to take us to the *matatu* station outside Kisumu.

"What in the world is a *matatu*?" Elaine asked as we all climbed into the taxis.

"A *matatu* is ah, uh . . . well, let's say it's an *unusual* type of African transport. The name comes from a saying that

'There is always room for three more people in a *matatu*,' "
I said grinning, knowing full well that *tatu*, or "three," is an
understatement.

Only a few minutes later we were suddenly thrust into
bedlam at the Kisumu country bus station. A confusing mass
of monstrous, beat-up, blaring, honking, psychedelic-colored
buses were roaring in and out of the station blasting up more
dust, petrol fumes, ear-shattering racket, and clouds of black
smoke than the London blitz. It seemed fit that each purple,
yellow, or green dinosaur of a bus had a weird name plastered
circus truck-style across the sides: "Attaway To Go," "Simba
Express," "Moon Rocket," and "Apollo Launch." Luggage
piled as high as Kilimanjaro swayed ominously on top of the
roof racks that were laden with bicycles, mattresses, bed-
springs, boxes of live chickens, and burst sacks of maize meal
snowing down past the windows. The bus drivers' helpers,
called "turnboys," were hanging precariously out the doors
or on the rear bumpers, hollering and banging their hands
against the bus sides, trying to attract more passengers.
Crowds of noisy vendors were hawking live chickens, fruits,
and peanuts. This riot looked more like a mass evacuation
from a disaster than a bus station.

My companions just sat in the taxis struck dumb by this
wild carnival atmosphere. When we removed the bags from
the taxis, my friends were aghast when Margaret pointed out
a weird-looking contraption on wheels. Listing to starboard,
a mini-sized pickup truck, with a tiny metal cabinlike struc-
ture fastened onto the truck bed, came careening into the
station. There were so many Africans inside the tiny cabin
that it looked as though they had been welded together, layer
upon layer, their faces pressed against the windows. "*That*'s
a *matatu!*" Margaret announced. "And that's our transport
to Homa Bay."

It was incredible that a *matatu*, not much bigger than a
pickup camper, could hold so many people. Its top-heavy
luggage rack threatened to topple over the entire vehicle.

When the *matatu* shuddered to a stop, some thirty passengers or so disembarked like a scene from the classic circus act where an endless stream of clowns emerges from a toy car. It is no wonder that a *matatu* is nicknamed "the cupboard."

"Don't worry," Margaret encouraged my wide-eyed companions. "There'll be room for us."

Once our bags were hoisted up onto the *matatu*'s roof rack, the springs creaking from Elaine's bag, the rear door of the *matatu* gaped open and we were slowly swallowed up inside. Our seats were nothing more than an empty rock-hard metal bench. So far, not so bad, until we realized that we were not to be the only passengers. Within minutes, a few Africans began to climb in and sit next to us on the bench. Then, like an assembly line, more Africans entered as we moved down the bench one by one. We scrunched together to make room for another and another and another. Our hips were squeezed so tightly together that we felt as though we were in a junkyard car compactor. When the U-shaped bench was packed with people, still more crammed in. Some African women carried small, naked, round-faced babies.

"Who gets to sit next to the birds?" I heard Elaine whisper just as an old man climbed in holding two clucking chickens. Additional passengers entered but had to stand up trolley-style, holding onto metal handles on the ceiling. When two "Mamas" could find no room for their babies, they promptly set them on Pete's and Brian's laps, much to the delight of the Africans. I now counted thirty-six people inside "the cupboard."

When the "turnboy" finally got the door shut, he banged against the *matatu* sides to signal we were ready to go. The tortured tearing of gear shifts and the screaming engine jerked us onto the main road, bucking us along like a broncobuster at a rodeo. Soon we were racing along the road, our spines rattling like castanets. We began passing a dilapidated purple bus with broken windows, bald tires, and wheels wobbling crazily, threatening to tear loose at any moment. We stared with alarm at the bus's partially caved-in roof—and then noted the huge sign painted on the bus's side: WE SEEK GOD.

Having had so much experience traveling on rural transport, Margaret told a fascinating story. "One night I was bumping along the dirt roads on a large country bus named 'Owya Baby,' when suddenly a frenzy broke out on the bus. Passengers were shouting and trying to climb over the seats. The bus quickly stopped and people started surging toward the door. I was confused, and it was only when I walked to the bus door that I learned that there was a snake on board! I, too, alighted and watched the unfolding scene. Someone then knocked the large snake out the bus door with a stick, and I was later told it was a very poisonous snake. As we continued on our journey, two elderly Luo women reached forward in their seats behind me and waved their hands excitedly and called out to me, 'Mama Mzuri! Mama Mzuri!' I felt panic, thinking I might have upset them somehow. But the young woman next to me explained that they were only praising me for being so brave during the commotion. How could I tell them it was only the lack of awareness, and not bravery?"

Several hours later we were only a few minutes from Homa Bay town. As we bumped along the corrugated road, suddenly a commotion broke out inside our *matatu*. The Africans began to laugh, pointing to the shocked, red faces of Brian and Pete whose pants legs were soaked. The two naked babies, flashing toothless grins, had happily relieved themselves on their laps.

# 5

IT WAS LATE AFTERNOON when the *matatu* rumbled onto the dusty streets of Homa Bay town, lined with its gaily painted shops called *dukas*. Like children's giant toy blocks, each *duka* was slapped with a dazzling coat of either blue, pink, green, purple, or red paint. Painted onto the *dukas'* outside walls—and done by local, self-taught artists—were giant jungle scenes picturing baboons drinking Coca-Cola, two elephants with trunks entwined holding a bottle of Tusker beer, and a seven-foot tall chicken advertising Rooster cigarettes. Painted above a doorway of a local bar with a disco—where a rinky-tinky, toe-tapping tune was blaring from an old juke box—was a primitive-looking Mickey Mouse doing a crazy jitterbug with Minnie. All over East Africa, *duka* towns everywhere reflect the spontaneity and originality of African artists.

We rattled to a stop at the *matatu* station, and then like circus contortionists, we tried to straighten out our twisted limbs and tortured spines before climbing out of "the cupboard." Several eager young Luo boys raced up to Margaret to carry our bags up a hill to her house. We would rest there until morning when Jack and the African driver would arrive with the vehicles to continue our journey to the big game country of the Masai Mara plains. On Christmas Eve we would be pitching our tents right among the great migrating herds of the Serengeti; on New Year's we would be climbing toward the snows of Kilimanjaro.

As the boys took one path to carry our bags to the house, we followed Margaret on another path to climb the steep, conical-shaped Asego Hill, several hundred feet above the bay. A short while later, we were standing on top of Asego to take in a sweeping view of this African Shangri-La. Clusters of round, thatched dwellings, and a few rectangular, iron-roofed houses dotted the verdant hills that rolled down to the papyrus-lined shores. The landscape was broken up by golden patches of maize fields, surrounding small farm plots called *shambas*, where tiny human figures could be seen working their way through the maize stalks. Barely distinguishable on the horizon, a flotilla of small fishing *dhows* bobbed up and down in the sparkling blue waters where Luo fishermen cast their nets for Nile perch and tilapia, a succulent gourmet fish.

Some four centuries ago, the Luo tribe's ancestors were pastoralists, having migrated with their cattle along the Nile to the largest lake of the Rift Valley. Gradually, however, the Luo (then known as the Kavirondo) settled down and became fishermen, and began to grow crops. The introduction of maize to Africa from the New World—believed to have been first brought in the 1500s by the Portuguese—eventually spread all over Africa to become the main staple crop for agriculture on the continent.

"As inviting as the bay waters appear," Margaret said, "they do hold potential hazards for the people. Tiny snails that live in the reeds close to shore carry a blood fluke known as bilharzia, a parasite that infects a person's bladder, turning the urine bloody red. Most Luo people suffer from it, and those with the worst untreated cases have died from it. The Peace Corps doctors try to help with newer medicines, but since there are over 2.5 million Luo, it is impossible, of course, to reach everyone. And there are the dangers from the hippos that hide in the papyrus reeds during the day. At night they sometimes wander onto land to graze on the small farm plots known as *shambas*. Hippos are exceptionally dangerous if you happen to get between them and their escape route back to the water. Despite its two-ton weight and stumpy legs, a hippo can easily run down a man. There have been many incidences where a hippo has literally chomped a man in two with its massive jaws and twenty-inch-long ivory teeth. Not long ago here in Homa Bay, a game warden shot a menacing hippo. It was then butchered and the meat and fat divided up for scores of families whose crops were trampled by hippos.

"It's getting late," Margaret said, "so we'd best get to my house before sunset. You all need some rest before driving over those corrugated roads tomorrow to the Mara game country." As we descended the hill, Margaret said that though food sources appear plentiful in Homa Bay, the Luo people, like most Africans, have to struggle to survive. Kenya has the highest birth rate in the world, and consequently food production can barely keep pace with so many more mouths to feed each year. In the drier areas of East Africa, the people survive on little more than a porridge made from maize meal called *ugali*. Even in the more productive areas such as Homa Bay, life is a treadmill. The Luo fishermen must work seven days a week. The women—seen working in the fields with their babies strapped onto their backs—till the soil with antiquated tools from dawn to sunset.

Even though old traditions govern their daily lives, most Africans are eager to learn different methods in which to best help themselves. This is one of the reasons the Peace Corps is a success in Kenya with programs for improving crop productivity, reforestation projects, water conservation, health care, and skilled trade instruction. Education is the key factor, and was Margaret's reason for being in Homa Bay. Soon after her arrival, several Luo women urged her to set up a nursery school. There was no precedent for a nursery school in upcountry Kenya, and virtually no money for such a project. Margaret was faced with a challenge.

Eventually an old, one-room stone building was donated; then Margaret and several Luo women went to work to create a school with handmade furnishings. Since there were no supplies or toys, the old adage "necessity is the mother of invention" applied perfectly; banana leaves were fashioned into dolls, sisal fiber into jump ropes, tin cans hammered into toy *matatus*. Sticks, bottle caps, and beanbags became "instruments" for a children's rhythm band. When the school opened they initially had twenty-four children, who quickly learned English from the nursery rhymes and stories. Activities in art, music appreciation, and craft-making broadened their world. The school became such a success that plans were put in motion to construct a permanent building for the Asego Hill Nursery School. Margaret had introduced the concept of early childhood education in Homa Bay—the first of its kind in East Africa.

A half hour later we approached Margaret's bungalow-style house and entered its musty rooms. Like most Peace Corps volunteers, Margaret lived modestly with Spartan furnishings of a few chairs, tables, bookcases, bathroom, and a kitchen made up only of a sink and a tin, charcoal-burning stove called a *jiko*.

After Margaret had brought tea and sandwiches, we sat on her veranda to watch a bloodred sunset reflect in the bay. Near the equator there is virtually no twilight, and the landscape was quickly plunged into darkness. Pinpoints of lantern lights flickered on across the hills like fireflies.

"Are you ever afraid to be alone here at night?" Elaine asked as Margaret lit kerosene lamps, and we all prepared to roll out our sleeping bags on the floor for the night.

"Never," Margaret said. "I feel protected by these gentle people who watch over this older American woman who teaches their children. I think of their generosity, giving you fish or a chicken, to show thanks. I see little brothers and sisters walking hand in hand, watching out for one another. I know that the Luo people must change, as they face the twenty-first century. But sometimes at night, when I sit on the veranda, I silently cry to myself and whisper a hope for the Luos: 'Don't change completely. Keep your sweet, guileless ways—you, who count your family and friends as your true wealth above all treasures.' "

At dawn, we rose and headed into town for breakfast at a *duka*. Just as we had finished eating, we were excited to see Jack and the African driver come roaring into town with the overloaded safari vehicles stirring up dust and chickens. When we waved down Jack, he pulled the Land Rover up to the *duka* with the van close on his heels. "We need coffee!" a bleary-eyed Jack said. "My African friend and I have driven all night."

While Jack headed into the *duka* for breakfast, the gang and I began hoisting our bags up onto the Land Rover's roof rack—and securing Elaine's bag with extra rope. A little later, Margaret returned from the fish market with her Kenya basket filled with several bundles wrapped in newspapers. "Because tomorrow is Christmas Eve, I thought I would give you something special," she said, unwrapping the papers to show us several pounds of fresh tilapia, which we promptly put in the Dry Ice coolers.

"I think we'd best get a move on," Jack said as he stepped out of the *duka*. He paid the African driver, who would take a bus back to Nairobi; Brian and Pete would take over the driving of the safari van.

Before climbing into the vehicles, we thanked Margaret for showing us this other side of Africa. She had inspired us with the fact that a person with unwavering idealism and tenacity—young or older—*can* make a difference in the world. As we pulled out of town, we looked back to see Margaret heading back up the hill to her nursery school, trailed closely by a group of Luo children.

To give Jack a little "breather," I had taken over the driving of the Land Rover. Everyone was in high spirits, full of anticipation, as we jounced along the washboard roads under the wide-open Kenya skies. We drove for a long distance southward, then turned east for the 100-mile journey to Masai Mara Reserve. Ulla, Aya, and Elaine were riding with Jack and me, while Brian and Pete brought up the rear in the van.

"Hey! We'll have to turn back to Nairobi immediately!" Elaine kidded us. "We forgot the Christmas decorations!"

"From the looks of that duffel bag of yours," Jack piped up from the back seat, "I thought you'd packed the Christmas *tree*."

Elaine was determined that we must have a proper Christmas celebration on the Serengeti Plain, and said she'd improvise something.

After we drove many hours on the rocky roads, the *shambas* of western Kenya began to thin out as we approached the drier, sparsely populated open country near the Masai Mara Reserve. By late afternoon, we suddenly reached the dramatic sheer-drop overlook of the Oloololo escarpment. Hundreds of feet below, the undulating green hills of Masai Mara disappeared into what Ernest Hemingway called "miles and miles of bloody Africa." There was no sign of civilization. This is the country where Hemingway hunted in 1934, and later wrote of his adventures in his classic *Green Hills of Africa*.

The sun would be setting in a couple of hours, so we decided to move quickly on so as to be at the ranger's gate before closing time. Working our way down the steep escarpment road, we made it to the ranger's post with only twenty minutes to spare; the gates close at 6:30 P.M. sharp. The park rangers, dressed smartly in their starched green uniforms and kepis, urged us to hurry to a camping place before dark.

The fast-fading light was making the driving risky, since you begin to see imaginary giraffe and gazelle in front of you, as well as the real thing. As soon as you enter African game country the pulse quickens, wondering what might suddenly appear on the track ahead. No place on earth gets the adrenalin flowing faster than the African plains. It was a free feeling, being completely self-sufficient with supplies. Even if we should have a major mechanical breakdown at night, within a couple of hours our camp could be set up and we could sit down to a gourmet meal in the middle of the bush.

We were anxious now to reach a place to camp before nightfall. All of a sudden there was a loud bang, and I began struggling with the steering wheel, trying to keep the Land Rover on keel. "Tires always find the most opportune time to blow," grumped Jack as we came to a stop. We all piled out of the car and saw the right front tire flat to the rim. The van pulled up behind and Brian and Pete began to lend us a hand. Then in the dimming light, we grumbled as we jacked up the Rover. By this time, we were all tired and hungry.

Aya tapped me on the shoulder. "I think we have company," she said, pointing to a black cluster of shadowy, bulky figures a hundred feet off the side of the road—Cape buffaloes. The herd looked like immovable boulders, and the black outlines of their huge upswept horns reminded me that buffaloes are not to be trifled with. Most of the old-time hunters considered the bull buffalo to be the most dangerous of the big game because it is preternaturally cunning. A one-ton bull can charge at nearly 30 miles an hour; its massive boss of horns can even deflect a bullet. If a buffalo is wounded by a hunter, it will disappear into the brush, and then with uncanny presence of mind, stealthily stalk the hunter from behind. When a buffalo gores a man, it is unrelenting in pulverizing its victim into a bloody pulp.

Keeping that image in mind, it was amazing how quickly we changed the tire. Buffaloes in herds usually do not create a threat—it's those lone bulls you watch out for.

The new tire on, we were off again, following now the beams of our headlights as darkness was upon us. A short while later, our headlights shone onto an open space surrounded by a few acacia trees. We had found our campsite.

We at once put our teamwork into motion as we unloaded the vehicles. Jack set up our two high-powered lamps that are generated from our car batteries. Once the tent boxes were off the roof rack, I boasted to everyone that I had purchased new nylon tents that would save us time for assembly. Rather than having to use hammers to pound in stakes and connect endless guy wires, the nylon tents use a color-code system of interconnecting poles. Assembly was to be a snap—and we'd soon be enjoying cold drinks and our dinner. I had failed to mention that I had never bothered trying out the system and that the tents were still in their factory boxes.

Taking the tents and poles out of their boxes was the easy part. I then stood under the acacia trees reading Jack the directions by flashlight. "Now, let's see," I started, as our companions set up their canvas chairs to watch. "The long red outside support poles connect with the shorter orange tent roof poles. Once those are in place, you connect the orange poles to the shorter yellow poles which support the center. You lock those in place and then attach the long center poles with the green stripes to the maroon-striped eaves poles and then . . ." It didn't help matters that Jack could not see the colors well in the lamplight, and he was quickly losing his patience. I made a furtive glance at my companions sitting in their chairs, glumly staring at me like five Jack Bennys. Somehow the pictures on the direction sheets did not match up with the way the tent was being assembled: one side of the tent looked fully inflated, the other side looked as if it had just sprung a leak and was slowly deflating. My tired and hungry companions were not amused.

"I think this needs a woman's touch," Aya interrupted as she rallied Ulla and Elaine—and they at once took over. Working away like little elves, with Elaine reading the directions, the tent sprung to life as easily as children assembling a well-loved toy. Within thirty minutes or so, the other six tents were up. As they stood back to admire their work, Aya crowed, "You see. Easy as a snap! Tomorrow you guys get to put up the tents. I hope you were watching closely."

Jack, Pete, Brian, and I began to set up the large collapsible dining table, stands, and safari kitchen equipment of propane stove and burners, pots and pans on the cook's table, and poured water from the jerry cans into smaller containers. Since it was too late to get a campfire going for cooking, we would use the propane stove. We then removed the two large Coleman coolers from the van for easy access to the food.

Since Elaine was our *mpishi*, or cook, she began to organize the utensils, pans, cooking oil, spices, and other items needed for her work on the cook's table. Aya and Ulla were already busy cutting up the vegetables. When I removed the fresh fish from the coolers, Elaine pointed out the delectable, pinkish-white tender flesh of the tilapia fillets.

Elaine insisted on doing up the dinner preparations as if we were at a fine Manhattan restaurant: red tablecloth, a meticulously set table with plates, silverware, folded napkins, water glasses, and even candles—which, of course, she had brought along in her bag.

Once the candles were lit, and several kerosene lanterns placed on the table, we turned off the bright floodlights that had been attracting too many bugs. We were blinded for a few moments as pitch-blackness enveloped the campsite. When our eyes finally adjusted to the dark, we watched the Milky Way splatter thick white paint across the vast night sky. One is always stunned by the sheer brightness of African stars that appear like shattered crystal at the moment of impact.

By this time the enticing aroma of tilapia frying in butter and frying potatoes wafted through the night air from Elaine's kitchen. Fifteen minutes later, Elaine, Aya, and Ulla brought platters of a five-course dinner: celery mushroom soup; tossed salad; tilapia smothered in butter and mild spices; French fried potatoes; fresh fruit cocktail; and cheese. We applauded Elaine as she started to take her seat at the candlelit table. She bowed demurely, and said, "Let's dive in!"

We all believed that tourists miss something when they are confined to lodges, electric lights, and noisy crowds at a bar. As we dined under the stars, little had changed in the spirit of those safaris of the 1920s and '30s. At one time, the Mara plains was one of the most favored hunting grounds during East Africa's safari heydays. When British East Africa was officially designated Kenya colony in 1920, an era of what was dubbed "champagne safaris" was ushered in that lasted throughout the twenties and thirties. The richer the clients in those days, the more luxurious the safari trip. The introduction of the automobile transformed safari companies into opulent affairs with fleets of Safari Fords, Willys-Knights, and Dodge Power Wagons that saved days of travel to the Mara or to Kilimanjaro. No expense was spared with other equipment that included tents covering an acre of ground, generators for lights, and refrigeration in zinc-lined trucks. The professional white hunter was the iron-handed camp boss over a retinue of drivers, trackers, gun bearers, skinners, *cordon bleu* African chefs (preparing everything from escargots and chicken Kiev to exquisite chocolate soufflés), a servant to warm the clients' baths, and a waiter to chill the champagne. No bill was too large to fill, although there were some weird requests. When a 375-pound Oriental prince could not waddle through the bush on his trophy hunts, one ingenious hunter solved the dilemma. He rigged up a one-wheeled rickshaw to transport his roly-poly plutocrat down the game trails. In 1928, one "champagne safari" firm mounted an expedition for the Prince of Wales (later King Edward VIII); another safari company guided the Duke and Duchess of York (later King George VI and his queen consort). The "dean of white hunters," Philip Percival, guided Ernest Hemingway on his hunts across the Mara plains.

"Well, we may not be royalty," Elaine said, passing extra helpings of tilapia as we discussed the old safari days, "but we seem to be doing okay—and doing it a heck of a lot cheaper."

After cleaning up after our dinner, we wanted to retire early so as to get an early start the next morning. We planned to pitch our camp in the Serengeti by late afternoon to make our preparations for a Christmas Eve celebration. Once we finally crawled into our respective tents, I lay awake for some time listening to the syncopated rhythms of insects, and the ghostly calls of a hyena far in the distance.

Several hours later, I was awakened by hollow clomping on the ground, then the tearing and ripping up of grass. Night visitors on the hoof. Opening the tent flap, I switched on my flashlight—and there, about fifty yards away, were approximately 100 glowing orbs of buffalo eyes floating on the sea of blackness. Most likely it was the very same buffalo herd we had seen when we had changed the tire. The buffaloes were not intending any harm, only looking for delectable blades of grass. My companions had also been awakened, and we flashed our torches onto one another's tents—and with hushed signals warned that this would not be the opportune time to use the "bush toilet" behind a distant acacia tree.

Just before I drifted back to sleep, I heard Elaine peep from her tent, "I think I have to go to the bathroom—but I think I can wait."

# 6

JACK AND I WERE UP BEFORE DAYBREAK to begin preparing breakfast. We wanted everyone up early so as to be on the road to the Serengeti. Like a giant photo negative slowly developing, the Mara plains began to take form in the faint yellow light of dawn. Just before I got out the pots and pans, Jack called me over to his tent to show me something. Within only two feet of his tent flap opening, hoofprints of where a buffalo had walked at night were clearly visible. Jack had been so dead to the world catching up on nearly two days of no sleep that he had heard nothing.

After we finally got everyone out of their tents, we sat down to our bacon and eggs. Then the team reloaded the equipment into the vehicles and we were off. We soon arrived at the Kenya-Tanzania border post, and handed over our passports to the customs' official for stamping so that we could enter Tanzania. Although we now passed through a political boundary, the landscape was but a continuation of the Masai Mara, merging with the Serengeti Plain a little farther to the south.

As we rounded a bend, a harem of 55 impala emerged from the bush, wearing their brightest fawn colors in the early morning sun. Their spirits running high, the impala put on a ballet for us—weightless creatures sailing over one another, legs drawn up to cheat the wind and gravity.

Much later in the morning, we steered the vehicles over one more hill and now the golden-green savanna of the Serengeti drops to a bottomless depth before us. Only a few flat-topped acacias and islands of huge golden rock outcrops, called *kopjes*, add dimension to the iron-flat plains. The sun is now overhead, and shimmering heat waves undulate and waver in the distance—distorted mirages in blue and gold constantly overlapping.

We are lucky to be in the Serengeti now, since the awesome migrations of the wildebeest, antelope, gazelle, and zebra are at present taking place in the south-central sections of the park. We are still a hundred miles from the migrating hordes and anticipation rises within us.

Since it is Christmas Eve day, we decide to set up camp early in the afternoon near the central part of the park. We want to keep away from the Seronera Lodge to avoid the tourists. The hard-packed roads make driving amazingly smooth as we keep our eyes peeled for a suitable campsite. Luckily, because it is the Christmas holidays, we see only an occasional vehicle. We have the Serengeti practically to ourselves.

We spot a 100-foot-high golden rock outcrop several hundred yards off the track, and decide this would be the perfect place for our campsite. As we began to unload the vehicles at the base of the *kopje*, we kept in mind that rocky outcrops offer excellent places for concealment for snoozing lions, or a leopard that lies up during the heat of the day.

Once the tents were set up, we began to organize the food supplies for our Christmas Eve dinner. We had picked up bits and pieces of wood along the way to use for our campfire.

By late afternoon all of our equipment was set up. Elaine decided that no Christmas Eve would be complete without a Christmas tree. She peered around and then spotted a small thorn bush growing only a few feet from the openings of the tents. She eyed this scraggly, emaciated excuse for a tree, and in the next few minutes, she rummaged through her duffel bag and found our tree "ornaments."

Brightly colored Dixie cups were tied onto long strands of

grass and then strung onto the scrawny tree limbs. Elaine thought the thorn tree most indignant as it struck back at her with its six-inch long thorns. The tree finally surrendered to Elaine's determination and small Christmas balls fashioned from aluminum foil joined the "clop-clopping" Dixie cups in the wind. Here was one first that even Macy's department store had never thought of. We were all proud of that Christmas tree, making stars from aluminum foil, everybody adding their own "ornaments." The tree was a work of love and imagination.

Elaine soon got everyone coerced into helping put the safari kitchen in order. She mentioned that we would have surf and Serengeti turf: tilapia thermidor; enormous T-bone steaks (still frozen solid in the Dry Ice coolers); vegetable soup; shrimp cocktail (from a can); baked potatoes; salad; and a few surprises.

We were so engrossed in our work that before we knew it the red ball of sun was balanced on the horizon. In the dimming light we lit kerosene lanterns to set out on the table, meticulously spread by the gals. Brian and Pete soon had the campfire ablaze, while Jack and I wrapped large potatoes in aluminum foil and placed them in our campfire "oven." Then I removed seven huge T-bone steaks from the coolers, and put them on the campfire grate. Elaine was busy making a thermidor sauce for the tilapia consisting of canned thick cream, cooking sherry, red cayenne pepper, butter, and melted Parmesan cheese.

"I've got to have music while I cook," Elaine said as she disappeared to her tent and returned with her stereo tape player which she set on the cook's table. "You must hear my favorite song," she said, snapping in a cassette in the player. Johnny Mathis and a full orchestra played a lush rendition of "There is someone walking behind you . . . turn around, look at me." She played it over and over. We razzed her that her theme song in the African bush should be "There is some *thing* walking behind you."

Within the hour, platters for a seven-course dinner were set out on the candlelit table that would do any "champagne safari" credit. Since it was Christmas Eve, it was time for a blessing of the meal—and to give thanks for the privilege of being on the African plains at this special time. We then made a toast to the Serengeti with red wine before starting our steak and tilapia thermidor dinners.

After dinner, we all moved our chairs around the blazing campfire. Elaine played a tape of Handel's *Messiah*. It seemed, as we listened quietly, that we were hearing this beautiful inspired work for the first time. The warm red glow on our faces from the fire became the playground for arabesque quivering shadows. The Christmas tree glowed from the flickering candles that were placed in circular fashion around our camp and tree, while the Dixie cups danced in the wind. As the voices of the *Messiah* chorus exalted, almost burning themselves out in the triumphal "Hallelujah Chorus," the night surrounding us seemed larger and fuller. The depth between earth and stars was felt. We were suddenly smaller.

Later, we decided that no Christmas Eve would be complete without dancing. Our hurricane lamps were moved to make a large square, marking out a grassy dance floor. Elaine played tapes of Dionne Warwick, who kept singing about "little green apples" and "snow in Minneapolis." We had the first disco in the Serengeti. Were those hyenas laughing?

We returned to the table for coffee, and a Christmas pudding Elaine had prepared from custard and honey. The winds across the plains began to ruffle the camp, flapping and snapping the tents with great force. The clop-clop-clopping of the Dixie cups increased in tempo. We shone our flashlights out onto the plains, and the light just caught the dark forms of nine giraffe gathered around acacia trees about seventy-five yards from us.

Although little game was to be seen around the camp, tomorrow would be different. The southern part of the Serengeti would be black with game from horizon to horizon.

We would soon experience the greatest wild animal spectacle on earth, a scene little changed from the Pleistocene Age.

When we took our lanterns to return to our tents, a little surprise was awaiting us. Three of the tents had been blown over flat by the wind; the other four tents were also beginning to collapse. Aya went back to the tent bag, and started reading off the directions again: "Let's see, the long red outside poles connect to the orange poles that . . ."

Elaine was now wiping her eyes with Kleenex.

We had all overslept; the inside of my tent was bright with light, and my sleeping bag had become a sweaty, baking shell. When I emerged from my tent, I was surprised to see the herd of nine giraffe still browsing on the acacias on the periphery of the campsite. As harmless as a giraffe appears, it can defend itself with its huge platter-sized sharp hooves, kicking out with the power of a steam hammer. It is not unusual for a lion to be killed by a giraffe that defends itself or its young. The giraffes were just as surprised to see me materialize, and they stood stock-still, staring at me for several minutes, and then walked on. *Out of Africa* author, Isak Dinesen, described them perfectly: "A giraffe is so much a lady that one refrains from thinking of her legs, but remembers her as floating over the plains in long garbs, draperies of morning mist and mirage."

A while later, Jack and I had the breakfast going, and the smell of frying bacon aroused our sleepyhead companions. I reminded them to shake their shoes out before putting them on. Since shoes are left outside tents, it's a perfect opportunity for little critters to make an overnight stop. The red-hot sting of a scorpion on your toe is an unforgettable experience. I told my companions to check the stockings as well—Christmas morning or not.

Soon after we had breakfast, and had all the equipment loaded, we were off across the Serengeti. This was to be a memorable Christmas Day.

We had been reading the classic wildlife book, *Serengeti Shall Not Die*, written by Dr. Bernhard Grzimek of the Frankfort Zoo. In the late 1950s, Dr. Grzimek and his twenty-four-year-old son Michael had been the first to do an aerial scientific survey of the Serengeti. Using a single-engine, zebra-striped airplane, they flew transects across the then unmapped Serengeti and estimated the numbers of wildebeests, zebras, antelopes, and other plains game. They discovered that it was human encroachment, rather than poaching in the 1950s, that was the biggest threat to the Serengeti. The Grzimeks' best-selling book and an Academy Award-winning film made the world aware of the phenomenal migrations of hundreds of thousands of animals—and the urgency to protect the Serengeti for future generations. The Grzimeks played a major role in persuading the Tanzanian government to safeguard this wildlife ecosystem.

It is the seasonal rains which draw the plains animals together in such great numbers. From December until May, wildebeests, zebras, antelopes, and gazelles graze in the south-eastern plains during the rainy season. Then the herds travel westward into the woodlands, later moving north into the Mara plains. When the dry season ends in late November, the herds return back to the Serengeti. The zebras precede the wildebeests, thereby preparing the way by grazing on the coarse tops of high new grass, which allows the wildebeests to munch on the more nutritious medium-high grasses. Then, the wildebeests have left the very short grasses for the hundreds of thousands of gazelles and antelopes that are the last to follow.

We were soon to experience an event that relatively few people in the world have ever seen. We continued driving along a road about forty miles south of Seronera and not much game was found except for a few lonely hartebeests and a few Thomson's gazelles. The distant horizons of the plains lost their flat straight lines wavering in the midday sun. Stillness. The grass quietly flows in the breeze, empty of game.

From the dining room of Nairobi's old Ainsworth Hotel, one looks out onto a garden courtyard.

The Land Rover is shifted to four-wheel drive to maneuver through gooey mud on a jungle track.

The millions of flamingos that gather at Kenya's Lake Nakuru are called the greatest bird spectacle on earth.

The shores of Homa Bay on Lake Victoria, home of the Luo tribe.

Our Dixie cup Christmas tree in Tanzania's Serengeti Plain.

Margaret Chamberlin with children of the Luo tribe in front of the Asego Hill Nursery School. (Courtesy of Margaret Chamberlin)

Entering Masai country of northern Tanzania

A young Masai boy watches over his flock of goats on the plains.

Elephants in Kenya's Amboseli Reserve, with Mount Kilimanjaro in the distance.

Carrying 40 pounds on his head, a porter leads the way up the path on the lower slopes of Mount Kilimanjaro.

The torturous climb straight upward toward the peak is accomplished inch by agonizing inch through the snows of Kilimanjaro.

The saddle area of Kilimanjaro is a desert plateau between the two peaks: 16,890-foot Mount Mawenzi (seen here shrouded in mist) and 19,340-foot Mount Kibo.

Muslim woman hides her face behind veil as she walks along the narrow alleyways of Mombasa's Old Town.

This bright red starfish is only one of many species of colorful sea life found among the coral reefs of Kenya.

The massive square face of Ol Doinyo Sabachi looms over Kenya's vast Northern Frontier.

A refreshing dip in the crystal-clear water of the springs at Buffalo Springs Reserve provides escape from the horrendous desert heat.

We now wondered how such a massive number of animals could still be invisible.

But then the vehicles reach the top of a grassy hill—and now we disbelieve our eyes. The plains have become a shore, holding back a living tidal wave. We have suddenly been whirled back into the Pleistocene Age.

This massive blackness wavers and flows miragelike, creating a flat liquid surface, undulating and rolling like all great seas. Waves of a sound I have never heard before roll across the plains, filling our ears. Time has left us—the migrations are real.

The deafening honking and wonking of thousands and thousands and thousands of wildebeests cut into the wind. We try to proceed through the black tidal wave of wildebeests. As we drive down among the great herds, this black sea seems to part, like a seam torn straight down the middle. The honking and wonking overflows the limits of space. Back in the 1920s, Martin and Osa Johnson felt as though they were passing a flood of hundreds of thousands of honking Model A Fords.

As the huge herds part before our vehicles, splashes of dust explode behind the now galloping animals, fleeing in front of our motorized intrusion. We stop the vehicles, and step out onto the plains, hoping to make it all more real by being among them. One wildebeest, perhaps one of the leaders, does a dance in front of his herd, an invitation for his kind to follow. Now the ground shakes as thousands of wildebeests thunder in front of our vehicles. We know well the limitations of a camera. We are lost in the dust. But it is not only the dust we are lost in. We are children again.

We climbed back into our vehicles, and slowly drove through the herds. Soon we climbed a rise in the road, and another spectacle awaited us: spread out on the rolling plain was the unbelievable sight of a shimmering black-and-white illusion. Thousands of Burchell's zebras blanketed the plain, their blur of overlapping stripes dazzling the eye. As we drove among the zebras we knew that you have to see this to believe that such teeming multitudes of animals are still left on this planet.

It was when we had driven away from the great herds toward a small stand of acacias that we first spotted them. In the high grass it looked as if several golden rocks had been scattered about under the trees. That is, until one of the "rocks" stood up and faced our fast-approaching vehicles. A large full-maned lion stood his ground as we pulled the vehicles within twenty feet of a pride of thirteen lions. The lion's amber eyes blazed directly at our vehicles. Here was no zoo lion, but the lord of the plains. As we pulled the vehicles up closer, two lionesses got to their feet, curious about us. The other lions—some only youngsters—were lying flat on their backs, paws resting on distended bellies, dried blood on their muzzles. A zebra carcass lay several yards away.

The Serengeti lion, known for its flowing dark mane, easily tips the scales at 450–500 pounds. This feline killing machine can bring down a full-grown bull buffalo—and then drag the one-ton carcass across the plains. Yet it is the more agile 300-pound lioness that does most of the hunting.

This king before us gave a half-hearted snarl and then plunked himself back down to rejoin the siesta of his snoozing pride. This pride was living up to the lions' reputations for sleeping nineteen hours out of twenty-four. At night a pride is usually on the hunt, booming their roars across the plains. A lion's roar begins with a series of low grunts, his chest heaving like giant bellows, working up to a full-throttled roar that can be heard five miles away. Up close, the paralyzing roar could shake the paint off a battleship.

The abundance of life on the Serengeti is like a giant buffet table for the lions, leopards, cheetahs, hyenas, and other predators that help keep a balance of nature. Yet they hardly make a dent in the teeming multitudes. Most often the predators attack the old, the sickly, or the young of the wildebeests, zebras, and gazelles. The most relentless of predators are the wild dogs that hunt in packs, harrying a wildebeest or zebra for miles, and then ripping open the victim's belly while still on the run. Nature gives the wildebeest calves a miraculous chance for survival: within only eight minutes after its birth, the calf will be on its feet and be able to run as fast as its mother to keep pace with the herd.

After driving a hundred miles from the migrations, we reached the outskirts of the Ngorongoro Conservation Area. Ngorongoro is a massive crater which is the largest volcanic caldera in the world. It is especially impressive since you come upon the deep crater bowl so suddenly. Before reaching the crater rim, we stopped the vehicles, got out and started to climb a small hill. After climbing for a few minutes, we reached the edge of the crater rim—and then abruptly we came upon a huge gaping cavity stretching some twelve miles across to the other side of the 360-degree rim. We peered down to the floor of the basin some 2,000 feet below us. Ngorongoro is so huge that it could contain the entire city of Berlin and all its suburbs. The crater is a whopping 250 square kilometres of woodlands and savanna that supports huge herds of wildebeest, zebra, buffalo, hippo, elephant—and even great numbers of flamingo in a soda lake. Ngorongoro has been called "the eighth wonder of the world."

We decided to camp on the crater rim for a couple of nights before heading for Mount Kilimanjaro. This would give us a chance to rest up before attempting Kilimanjaro's slopes. Our campsite on the crater rim was magic—especially at night when the waning moon over the crater bowl washed the amphitheater white, as if illuminated from within.

As peaceful as our camping nights had been, the distant roaring of lions one evening reminded us that unarmed humans are rather insignificant in the African wilderness. Several chilling incidents with campers in the past drove home the point that you can never throw caution to the wind. A tragic occurrence in the Serengeti several years ago wrote a bloody epitaph for one careless camper. Three men had been camping out on the plains, and because of the heat, one of the men decided to sleep with his head outside the tent. Long after the men had drifted off to sleep, two lions slunk through the shadows into the campsite. Snooping about, one of the lions spotted the man whose head was visible outside the tent flap—and instantly crunched its jaws down into the man's skull and began to drag him out of the tent. The man's terrified companions bravely shouted and threw camping items at the lions, who dropped the man and bolted out of camp. But sadly, the man died soon afterward.

Jack also had an experience that could have given him the *inside* view of a lion. A few months ago when we had been camping in another game reserve, I had retired to my tent where I fell fast asleep. Jack had been stretched out on a ground sheet near the campfire enjoying a drink, when he too drifted off into a slumber. Luckily, Jack's sixth sense must have been working well that night. The continuous soft rustling of the thorn trees was the only sound in camp, but something made Jack wake up. He opened his eyes and watched the thorny black arms of the acacias wavering above him, the outlines of the trees visible against the glitter of stars. He sat straight up and thought he saw a dark figure standing some twenty-five feet in front of him. Believing it was a client bending over to get something from a chop box, he switched on the flashlight—and instantly froze: a large lion stood before him, its eyes fixed like truck headlamps in the light of the torch. By reflex, Jack picked up a stone and pitched it in the lion's direction. Fortunately for Jack the lion did not want to play hard ball—and crashed off into the brush. The night after this, I noticed that old nonchalant, unflappable Jack moseyed off *into* his tent.

It was usually when we were careless in the bush that we stumbled into sticky situations. Within a few days' time, we would find ourselves in a frightening encounter with an elephant while walking outside our campsite in Amboseli Game Reserve.

# CHAPTER
# 7

THE MORNING WE LEFT Ngorongoro Crater for Kilimanjaro, our vehicles hit upon a hard rock road that led us to increasing numbers of Masai temporary compounds called *manyattas*. Scattered about the surrounding hills were large circular thorn enclosures for cattle corrals, and the Masai mud-and-dung huts that look like giant loaves of hard-baked bread. The Masai tribal grazing lands straddle the Kenya-Tanzania border where these pastoral people roam freely with their thousands of scrawny cattle, forever seeking greener pastures. For centuries, the Masai herders have shunned farming, looking down on agricultural tribes with contempt. Cattle have always been the center of Masai existence, providing them with everything they need: blood and milk for food, hides for bedding, mats, and sandals. The Masai believe that their god Ngai (who, they say, lives on Kilimanjaro) bestowed all the cattle in the world to the Masai alone. With such arrogant, self-imposed destiny, the Masai carried out cattle raids and made war on their neighbors.

In modern-day Africa when most tribes have abandoned their traditional customs and dress, the Masai remain stubborn anachronisms—colorful figures straight out of a nineteenth-century explorer's notebook.

Continuing for many miles along the jolting road, we passed groups of Masai women. They jangled along the roadsides like overdressed peacocks, bedecked in an excess of beaded jewelry and body adornments. The sheer weight of those draft horse-size collars—made up of endless strands of beaded necklaces—would bring a Budweiser Clydesdale to his knees. Coil after coil of copper bracelets were linked from wrist to shoulder, fitting as snugly as tourniquets. Earrings like barrel hoops stretched earlobes down to shoulders. "The latest agony of fashion," was the way Mark Twain once described Western dress styles. That would certainly apply to Masai fashion.

Elaine found it strange that these women who adorn practically every part of their body tossed away any notions of femininity in doing up their hair. Masai women shave their heads throughout their lifetimes. Elaine thought that perhaps since the Masai women spend so much time with their jewelry, they are too tired for anything else. But shaved heads for women are a Masai custom.

What the Masai women lack in hairdos, the junior warriors called *moran* make up for in elaborate pompadours. Each *moran* has his hair dressed by a fellow warrior who, with the precision and patience of a microsurgeon, braids each strand of hair into long plaits. This coiffure is then plastered with red ocher (a dye made from clay) and mutton fat. The process takes days—but the hairdo lasts for months—a Masai "permanent." The plaited tresses add panache to a warrior's regal, sculptured naked physique, draped only with a bloodred toga, his body painted with ocher. With catlike grace, the warriors stride across the grasslands with their long-bladed spears in hand.

But *warrior* is only a courteous title today, since there are no more tribal wars to be fought, and cattle raiding and ceremonial lion hunts are forbidden by the African governments. Less than a hundred years ago, the Masai warriors had a reputation for ferocity and courage unmatched by most East African tribes. So fierce were the Masai that even the ruthless Arab slave traders gave much of East African territory a wide berth. The Masai seemed indomitable until the late

1800s and early 1900s when smallpox, rapid European colonization, and famines sapped their power.

Bouncing along the road toward Arusha town, we passed a few government experimental agricultural and ranching schemes whose purpose is to settle some Masai clans into permanent communities. But we believed that forcing the Masai into an agricultural existence would be an assassination of their identity—an open-air prison for these freedom-loving people. Grass has always been their symbol of independence. Grass gave life to their cattle, and herding the cattle meant freedom to roam the plains, never chaining themselves to the tyranny of modern man's accumulation of material wealth—and ulcers. Grass was sacred, never to be broken for cultivation, nor the ground broken for burial. When a Masai dies, his body is placed in the open under a tree far from the *manyatta*. His sandals and cattle-herding staff are in one hand; in the other hand is a clump of grass. Not long afterward, the hyenas, vultures, and ants dispose of the body. An unsettling image for modern man, who tries to sweeten the reality of death, but the Masai have not forgotten one truth: we come into this world naked, and we go out of it naked.

Shortly before we reached Arusha town heading east, Aya and Ulla noticed a small, white solitary cloud suspended above the horizon. When we got closer to Arusha, the "cloud" revealed its true identity: the snows of Kilimanjaro. The flat-topped peak is exceptionally spectacular, since the four-mile-high mountain abruptly soars above the plains. Seeing snow on the peak, only a hundred miles from the equator, adds a sense of the unexpected. Mount Kilimanjaro is actually a volcanic massif that arose several million years ago, created from the geological process that formed the Great Rift Valley.

Kilimanjaro holds the record as the largest birthday present ever given. In 1886, Queen Victoria bequeathed the icing-topped mountain cake to the German Kaiser. Boundaries were redrawn around the mountain to incorporate Kilimanjaro into German East Africa. It was easier than moving the mountain.

A short while later, passing through Moshi town, we turned left on a road that led us into the large forest which completely skirts the mountain. Soon, the little mountain lodge of Kibo Hotel revealed itself nestled among the cedars and olive trees. Thin streams of smoke were spiraling up from the chimneys. When we parked the vehicles in the hotel's small side lot, we grabbed our bags and headed into the old hotel. A cozy little fireplace off the lobby took the chill out of the mountain air as it choked out wafts of tantalizing woodsmoke. An elderly German lady, who has run the hotel since the colonial days of old Tanganyika, greeted us and summoned two African porters to lead us down a dark narrow hallway to our rooms. The German woman was already instructing several Africans to begin preparing the camping and mountain gear provided by the hotel. She would also supply us with African porters to carry 40-pound loads each up the mountain.

After a filling supper of sausages and sauerkraut, we headed off to our ice-cold rooms to sleep. Luckily the beds in each room were piled high with huge, thick, wool blankets and sheepskin covers.

At the crack of dawn, Jack, Aya, Ulla, Pete, Brian, and I were already enjoying our breakfast. The windows in the dark dining room were covered with frost, giving us a preview of even colder temperatures to be endured up the higher slopes.

Elaine was in exceptionally high spirits—mainly since she'd be sitting this one out, curled up with a good book. "My creaking bones," she said, "would crack halfway up the mountain. Too many cold New Jersey winters."

After breakfast we began to help the porters with our mountain gear: heavy nailed climbing boots, bulky insulated parkas, gloves, sun goggles, Vaseline to smear on our faces for sun protection, small backpacks, and our walking sticks. The German woman said she had packed new sleeping bags that are made with some "miracle lining" for improved insulation, without the bulk of old sleeping bags. Sounded great to me.

Soon we were all ready, and walked out into the freezing dawn in our boots and parkas. The seven porters were just finishing checking the food in the chop boxes and checking off the camping equipment. Then the porters lifted the 40-pound loads up onto their heads, African-style, their traditional and sensible way to carry goods, permitting free movement of an arm. The African guide and three porters took the lead while three porters brought up the rear. Our trek would take us some seventy-five miles round trip. Three days up; two days down.

As the guide led the way through the forest with twelve eager figures following behind, we glanced up through an opening in the trees and were rewarded with a spectacular sight. Through the fading veil of mist, we saw the gleaming white face of Kilimanjaro looming above. From this distant view, the mountain looked an impossible climb.

Feeling like we were on a foot safari of yesteryear with our line of porters, we walked at a good, easy pace. Our first impressions as we started our trek was that this is the Africa one imagines—that is, except for the chilling temperatures. Our first day was rather easy except for the muscle strain as you begin to walk higher and higher up the slopes. Semitropical rain forest engulfs the path and the wall of trees is broken only by the thatched African huts and banana plots of the Chagga tribe who live on the forest slopes. Aya and Ulla bought bananas from some Chagga women, since we would need plenty of potassium for muscle strength. We'd have to drink five pints of liquid every day to prevent hypothermia and dehydration, and watch out for a nasty little thing called pulmonary edema, a high-altitude condition in which fluid passes into the blood and into the lungs. It is usually brought on when climbing too quickly—and can be fatal. We'd climb the slopes slowly.

As we walked up the forest path, many small African children followed us, laughing at our appearance in cloddy boots, and sunburned faces. We did not need a Chagga translator to tell us their laughter was one of derision and mockery.

Everyone and everything was soaked with mist, and it was now impossible to get a glimpse of the peak because of the density of the forest. But we knew it was still up there somewhere, challenging us to reach its 19,340-foot summit. The constant roar and trickling of invisible waterfalls and streams could be heard as we walked a little more to the vertical.

Our goal on the first day was to reach the first cabin, Bismark Hut, at 8,400 feet, which would be our sleeping quarters. As we climbed away from the villages, we practically tripped over some bowling ball-size droppings of elephants, the dry dung revealing that elephants had passed through here days ago. It was hard to imagine elephants roaming the freezing heights of 8,000 feet, but elephants somehow manage to navigate steep slopes, even reaching heights of 16,000 feet.

Kilimanjaro has always been connected with legends of African animals. The world's record ivory tusks were taken from an elephant shot on Kilimanjaro in 1897. Each tusk was eleven feet in length, and the combined ivory weight was 462 pounds. Leopards have been known to roam high up the mountain. In the 1920s there was the amazing story of a leopard that reached the alpine snow zone, an incredible 18,000 feet just below the peak. For many years, climbers told of seeing the mummified corpse of the leopard that had frozen to death. This so captured the imagination of Ernest Hemingway that he prefaced his classic story, "The Snows of Kilimanjaro," with this mystery: "Close to the western summit there is the dried and frozen carcass of a leopard. No one has explained what the leopard was seeking at that altitude." Eventually, climbers over the years cut off little chunks of frozen leopard for souvenirs until nothing remained but the legend.

As we continued to climb higher, the guide stopped in his tracks to point to what looked like a fallen log across the

path. On closer inspection we saw that the log was moving—
but it wasn't a log; it was a boiling mass of thousands of
safari ants called *siafu*. Moving close to take a photo, suddenly I laughed out loud when I saw laid-back Jack doing an
Irish jig on one leg at fast-forward speed. Several soldier ants
had found their way up Jack's pants legs—which we all
thought amusing until suddenly the rest of us joined Jack in
a wild whoop-hollering hoedown dance. A few extra ants had
found their way into our pants, too. With no thought of
modesty, we peeled off our jeans and tried to pluck the mean
little buggers out of our skin. Even though it took some time
to dig their pincerlike jaws out of flesh, a little rubbing alcohol
helped do the trick. Trying to regain some dignity by putting
back on our jeans, we then took flying leaps over the writhing
ant column and continued on our way.

Many of East Africa's early settlers told horror stories of
how millions of *siafu*, after the long rains, swarmed over
farmlands in waves, devouring practically every living thing
in their path. Some settlers had to abandon their farmhouses
as ants thick as black oily smoke boiled over the thatched
roofs, vacuuming up insects and rodents, spilling over into
living rooms and bedrooms. Many forewarned farmers prepared themselves by placing hot ashes around the farmhouses.
*Siafu* invasions were a living nightmare.

We did not come across any other *siafu* as we continued
to climb. Hours later we finally saw Bismark Hut a hundred
yards ahead through an opening in the trees. As is true when
you see your goal in sight, the climbing seemed impossible.
We swore that someone must have put the cabin on casters
and was slowly, teasingly, moving it farther away the closer
we approached. Even the now-visible mountain peak seemed
to be moving farther away. Kilimanjaro was fulfilling an old
Arab legend: "An enchanted mountain, which moves about,
which one seeks to reach and where no one ever arrives."

When we reached the cabin, we collapsed onto the bunks,
exhausted even more by the thin air at this altitude. Now the

porters made our ritual of steaming hot tea and biscuits. Heaven be praised for tea! There is nothing so reviving as this nectar of the gods. Refreshed, we stepped outside to watch the sun set. The resettling mist at the base of the mountain concealed most of the forest, but farther in the distance we could see a stretch of purple, yellow, and brown—the colors of the African plains—for endless miles.

At dawn we found ourselves on our way through an eerie forest of giant heath and trees draped with lichens and moss. Then, at 10,000 feet, we were startled when the forest abruptly ended, as though a giant scythe had cleared the edge of a forest wall in a straight line. We stepped out onto a moorland terrain, thick with fog, devoid of trees and carpeted with ankle-deep spongy grass and moss. It appeared a replica of Scotland's Highlands. The climb up Kilimanjaro is akin to walking from the tropics, across many latitudes of temperature and vegetation, all the way to the Arctic. Kilimanjaro is made up of five ecological zones: rain forest, heather, moorland, alpine, and summit of ice and glaciers.

We were blinded by the fog, and the porters walking ahead were swallowed up in the atmosphere. I stared down at my feet, as my boots sank into soft spongy moss, squish, squish, squishing with every step. The sensation was disorienting as though you were suspended in midair, floating through a cloud.

The second cabin, Horombo Hut, rests at 12,335 feet, and we still had some ten miles to go. Climbers many years ago often saw herds of elephants wandering over the moors. The only way you could see an elephant in this pea soup was to bump into one. The higher we'd climb, the less vegetation we saw. Certain species of plants would suddenly disappear within only feet of a certain altitude.

Around five in the afternoon, the clouds began to slide off the peaks to slowly unveil the mountain. You felt as if you could run up its side and touch the snow. It shone majestic, serene, crystal clear in the late afternoon sun.

Little did I know I would be willing to pay a king's ransom for a little warmth of the sun after we stumbled into Horombo Hut. After a light supper, and the porters had retired to their own hut, my companions and I crawled into our sleeping bags for a blissful night's sleep. When the sun goes down on "Killy," it's more than a bit chilly—it's numbing. After an hour passed, I was still cold. I asked my companions how they were doing, and they said "toasty warm." Of course, I thought, it takes awhile for the "miracle" lightweight lining on the new sleeping bags to heat up your body. Yes, that was it. Another hour passed and I was now freezing. Minutes later I began to lose all contact with my numbing fingers, toes, legs, and arms. I was convinced I was the only living body amputee in the world—just my head and pillow, alone together. Not bearing it any longer, I huffed outside to ask the porters in their cabin what was wrong with the "miracle" lining of the sleeping bag the German woman bragged about. Sheepishly, a porter solved the mystery: he had forgotten to zip in my "miracle" lining. It's a miracle I didn't kill him.

The next morning we left the hut early, following the path leading up to the 14,500-foot saddle area of Kilimanjaro. The saddle area is a flat desert plateau of loose sand and gravel, which lies between Kilimanjaro's two peaks: flat-topped Kibo and the shorter 16,890-foot peak, Mawenzi.

The walking is tolerable now on a horizontal plane that spreads out for miles. Hours later the path steepened and, in the distance, our eyes caught the flash of a tiny silver dot. It was the sun reflecting off the tin roof of Kibo Hut perched just below the snow line. Like bedraggled soldiers, propped up against one another, we finally hobbled into Kibo Hut and collapsed on the floor. It was not comforting to know that the porters would be waking us at 3:00 A.M. in order for us to make it to the summit by late morning. At 15,000 feet, we were already getting a taste of altitude sickness—nausea and sledgehammer-smashing headaches. Since it takes water longer to boil at high altitudes, we had to wait forever for our tea. Barely touching our suppers, we hit the sack with clothes on and tried to sleep. But the freezing temperatures left us shivering, teeth-chattering miserable wrecks. When we finally drifted off into slumber, we bolted awake when we thought we heard pistol shots. But it was only the rocks cracking as they cooled quickly from the warmth of the day. At high altitudes on "Killy," temperatures can fluctuate some 60 degrees from midday to midnight.

At 3:00 A.M. the guide and porters prodded at us as if we were corpses. When we finally got to our feet, we put on our thick, woolly parkas, had tea, then stumbled out into the darkness. Even in the icy starlight, Kibo glacier looming above us, that giant block of ice seemed to be made of phosphorescence. The sheer size of this peak had made it a beacon for Arab slave caravans threading their way through thick bush country. Several African tribes have attributed *Kili-n'-jaro* to mean "The Mountain of Caravans." When German missionary-explorer Johann Rebmann—the first white man to see Kilimanjaro, in 1848—told of seeing snow on a mountain near the equator, geographers back in Europe scoffed at him. But years later another explorer, Klaus von der Decken, explored Kilimanjaro's lower slopes and confirmed the existence of the glaciers.

As our own little caravan trekked more to the vertical in the freezing night, we quickly began to feel the effects of lack of oxygen. Talking was too much of an effort as we climbed silently upward. There was only the crunching of boots on rock and scree as we followed the wavering lights of the porters' kerosene lanterns. The fumes from the smoking kerosene added a bit to the nausea. Although we had three miles to climb, it would be straight up 4,000 feet. The guide behind me was always comforting me with the words *"po-lee, po-lee"*—slowly, slowly does it.

Real torture begins when we reach the edge of the snow level. The cold throbs through all your joints. Every muscle is rebelling against your every step, and lungs are expanded to full capacity, screaming for more oxygen as you approach 16,000 feet, constantly, mechanically moving one foot above the other. I felt like some poor puppet with its strings cut, suddenly collapsing in a heap, arms and legs in a labyrinth tangle.

We were resting more often now, leaning our backs against the ever-steepening slope. Throwing my head back against the scree, I was startled at the brightness of the stars that seemed to pull me inexorably into the heavens, tumbling me wildly through space. The clarity of the atmosphere in the night air was like nothing I had experienced before. The giddiness of altitude intensified the sensation of suspended animation.

Continuing on our way, we could just barely make out a large black hole in the mountainside: it was the entrance to Hans Meyer Cave (named after the man, who, in 1889, became the first to reach Kilimanjaro's highest peak). A half hour later, we followed the porters' lanterns inside the cave. We instantly fell onto our backs, eyes rolled back into our heads, mouths and jaws gaping and twisted into permanent grotesque gasps for air. Pete thought that we were all being prepared for burial.

An old African fable has it that this cave once held the treasures of King Solomon's mines. The legend tells of King Menelik I of Abyssinia (now Ethiopia)—the son of King Solomon and the Queen of Sheba—who hid his father's treasures and the gold seal ring in Kilimanjaro's caves. Anyone who finds King Solomon's gold seal ring will be bestowed with the wisdom of Solomon—and will restore Ethiopia to its former glory. These fables fascinated one English writer named H. Rider Haggard whose adventure story, *King Solomon's Mines*, was published in 1885.

As I looked around the cave, the only thing I was interested in finding now was an oxygen tank. Gradually, the cave began to lighten. Then, in slow motion, we pulled ourselves together, and "centimetered" our way to the cave opening. There was now only a hint of light on the horizon, but we were anticipating seeing a spectacular sunrise on old "Killy." The porters urged us out of the cave and told us we'd have to keep moving to keep warm. Then, as if in a dream, we started to climb straight up toward the peak.

Soon we were climbing in the snow, concentrating on every foothold, digging our steel walking sticks into the icy footing, continuously slipping backwards. The torturous efforts reminded me of a hamster on a wheel—we were going nowhere fast.

It was inch by inch above 19,000 feet, lungs heaving, hearts knocking against our chest walls. I realized that at this altitude jet planes fly, but with the benefit of pressurized cabins. My feet had become so numb that I felt as if I were wearing cement shoes. We tried not to look back down the dizzying sheer wall of snow and ice, but there were plenty of ledges wide enough to grab a foot- and handhold. Our muscles were beginning to turn to jelly as we reached out our gloved hands for a grip. Up and up, and 300 feet more to go. But as I looked up the wall of ice, it felt more like 300 miles walking on your fingertips.

We had to rest every minute or so, but the guide encouraged us on until our surrendering muscles lifted us that one more foot to the edge of the top of Kilimanjaro. When we reached the top, we keeled over on our backs and stared up into space. All thirteen of us were now temporary members in the most exclusive club in all of Africa: we were now the only people in the world atop the highest point on the African continent.

Momentarily, yellow light began to dissolve the blackness surrounding the mountain. Gradually, the icy sharp face of Mawenzi peak in the distance, below our gaze from Kibo peak, blushed pink, then a deep crimson, the entire mountain aglow. The horizon lifted like a lid over a giant fiery-red cauldron through the dusty atmosphere. On rare clear days after the rains, the atmosphere washed clean, it is possible to see 350 miles into the distance. At such a height, you are able to see the curvature of the earth.

For the next several hours we walked along the top of Kibo, and marveled at the blue-green masses of glaciers within the crater. We believed such a sight had made each agonizing step worth the whole journey.

After spending some time absorbing the view of Africa below our feet, we then reluctantly began our descent. Hours later, when our ankles were about to give in, we finally made it back to the hut we had left in the wee hours in the morning. I turned around and looked straight up at the alabaster face of Kilimanjaro—the mountain the Africans call *Nyumba ya Kumba*, The House of God.

# 8

Two days later our Kilimanjaro climbing party, nearly unrecognizable with sun-cracked faces, stumbled into the Kibo Hotel lobby where Elaine greeted us.

"Well," she said, "I see that the porters didn't have to carry you down from the mountain."

My climbing companions and I were dragging our tail feathers, shuffling along in our mud-caked gear, and sprouting garlands of the Everlasting Mountain flowers on our heads—gifts from our porters for our "triumph." We looked like lost Flower Children from the 1960s.

"And we probably smell like we've been dead for five days," grumped Jack as we staggered to our rooms for baths.

For two hours, I languished in a steaming tub and was close to soaking myself to death. When I emerged from my wallow, I looked like an albino prune. Eventually, we all gathered around the cozy, crackling lodge fireplace and re-galed Elaine with our adventures.

"You've had it too easy, Orange Blossom," Jack teased Elaine. "In a couple of days we'll put you back to work to make that 'mean spaghetti' you boast of. But if your pasta isn't a raving success, we leave you behind for the *mean* elephants of Amboseli."

Since our leg muscles had been mummified like the legendary leopard up the mountain, we decided to rest a couple of nights at Kibo Hotel to "recharge our batteries."

Two mornings later we were off in our vehicles winding up the eastern slopes of the mountain toward the Tanzania-Kenya border. The landscape gradually leveled out as we reentered the bush country of northern Tanzania and southern Kenya. After checking in at the border customs hut, we drove on into Kenya and reached the little tin shack town of Oloitokitok. It was here where Ernest Hemingway was based for a few months in 1953, performing duties as an honorary Amboseli Game Reserve warden.

It was a sweltering afternoon as we stirred up dust, rumbling down the wide dirt street lined with the square, tin-roofed *dukas*, looking much like a cow town of the Old West. Africans sat on the small porches of the *duka* shops that sold everything from Rooster cigarettes and Kimbo lard to Omo-brand washing powder and warm Cokes. Reaching the end of the *duka* town, two Land Rovers steered straight for us, the passengers waving for us to stop. Pulling up alongside us, two British couples quickly stepped out of their Rovers and started to rattle off at once. They wanted to ask if we were planning to camp in Amboseli since, only hours ago, their campsite had been completely flattened by a herd of sixteen elephants. Fortunately, the couples had been away on a game drive when the elephants barged into the campsite in the morning. Returning to the campsite later, they were horrified to find an elephant family destroying all camp equipment. The elephants had been looking for more food, already having consumed the fruit and vegetables left inside the now-flattened tents. In the process, everything had been demolished, and one elephant had managed to thrust her tusk clear through a Coleman cooler. The only thing the Britishers could do was watch helplessly as expensive equipment was turned topsy-turvy.

Jack and I were not surprised, since we knew that the

elephants of Amboseli were becoming bolder because careless campers left food accessible to them and to troops of baboons and vervet monkeys. Park authorities might soon close all campsites.

Thanking the young couples for their warning, Jack and I asked our companions if they wanted to risk camping for a few nights in Amboseli Game Reserve. Elaine reminded the others that we came for adventure, and we should take our chances. So we all agreed and headed off for Amboseli, never once suspecting a terrifying elephant encounter awaited us the next morning.

Soon after entering through Amboseli's rangers' post, the landscape became flatter, and the white soda plain was like confectioner's sugar-dust, permeating every crevice of the vehicles. There was no escaping it. Small tornadoes of dust—called "dust devils"—whirled and gyrated madly across the plains. The Africans aptly named these plains *amboseli*, meaning "salt dust." The choking atmosphere was churned up even more by the Masai, who bring their large herds of cattle into the Reserve seeking permanent watering areas near the swamps. The increasing numbers of Masai cattle herds in the Reserve are gradually turning Amboseli into a dust bowl.

Since Kilimanjaro is such a spectacular backdrop to Amboseli, the area has always been a popular movie location—for such films as *The Snows of Kilimanjaro, The African Lion, Where No Vultures Fly*, and many others. We wondered how Hollywood location crews were able to keep the white dust out of the huge Technicolor camera and sound equipment. Even double-sealed plastic bags couldn't keep the dust from penetrating our cameras.

We followed the burnt-out dry track roads toward the Loginya Swamp where great herds of elephants congregate. We would certainly see many herds moving in and out of the swamps near our campsite.

By late afternoon, we found a stand of acacia trees as the

ideal campsite because it faced Kilimanjaro. Although it was only thirty-some miles away as the crow flies, a bank of clouds engulfed the peaks and lower slopes for most of the day. Directly behind us, not far from this stand of acacias, was the wall of greenery that edged the Loginya Swamp.

Our companions were now like old circus hands, easily raising the tents, preparing the equipment for the safari kitchen, rigging up the portable shower on a limb of a distant acacia tree. The traveling circus was the right image with trucks, tents, canvas, portable kitchen, and living the gypsy life. The menagerie was all around us.

Since the Dry Ice had given up the ghost some time ago, Orange Blossom would be improvising meals from canned meat, rice, noodles, pasta, or whatever else she could dream up with her genius. Tonight was to be Italian Night with Elaine's "mean spaghetti" and a few other surprises.

While the others assisted with camp work or helped Elaine, it was my turn to head off for the shower with my soap, shampoo, towel, clean clothes, and a water jerry can. When I reached the open "Acacia Shower Room," I lowered the canvas bucket and poured a gallon or so into it, and then hoisted it about seven feet off the ground. By using the plastic clothespin "spigot," I turned on the shower. It always worked perfectly. There is nothing more refreshing than showering in cool water in the middle of the African bush, sweat and dust sloughing off as a dry breeze "towels" you off. Putting on a fresh cotton shirt and shorts, I felt as if I were wearing a new skin.

After Elaine went for her shower, Aya and Ulla complained that Orange Blossom was taking too long, most likely adding some orange "ocher" to her hair.

When everyone had freshened up, Elaine put us all to work to help with her Italian meal. It was "bubble, bubble, toil and trouble" as one pot on the campfire started to boil over with tomato sauce. Garlic bread was wrapped in aluminum foil and placed in the campfire oven. And, of course, while Elaine was preparing her salad in her kitchen, Johnny Mathis was singing "Turn Around, Look at Me" once again.

A short while later, like a line of waiters at a Roman feast, we carried the platters of steaming pasta to the table. The huge pot of gurgling spaghetti sauce sat as big as the *Queen Mary*'s boiler in the middle of the table. As we took our seats, we watched the red disk of sun slice down through the horizon and disappear. The sky caught fire with wavering crimson-and-gold flames of light.

Orange Blossom had not disappointed us. We heaped our plates high with spaghetti, and ladled on Elaine's tomato sauce made with every Italian spice imaginable and several assorted cheeses. Then we piled on the garlic bread and tossed salad. The dinner was enhanced with a bottle of Chianti. Not even Maxim's in Paris could match the atmosphere and taste of great food on the plains in the African evening. We stuffed ourselves like hippos on holiday.

A couple of hours later after our dinner, we sat at the table enjoying Elaine's improvised cappuccino. Then, just faintly, we thought we heard the distant trumpeting of an elephant. The sound had come from the direction of the swamp behind us. We got up from the table, grabbed our powerful torches and flashed them onto the black wall of grass 100 feet behind our camp. As beams of light probed between the acacias and openings in the grass wall, we could see nothing. Only the raucous din of insects revealed any presence of life. We knew that the elephants were fairly near, but staying, hopefully, in the swamp for the night.

We returned to the table to wash the dishes and stash the leftover food into the vehicles. We didn't want to tempt any elephantine appetites.

Once all the food and equipment was tidied up, we moved our chairs several yards away from the periphery of campfire light. When our eyes adjusted to the dark, we were excited to see that clouds had moved off Kilimanjaro, some thirty miles in the distance. The black outline of the huge sugar lump mountain was framed by the white path of the Milky Way—appearing to spume from the mountain itself.

Hearing the distant trumpeting again, we knew we'd have to take a bit more caution when using the "bush toilet" at night. Emerging from your tent to suddenly see an animal the size of a house only twenty paces away adds a whole new meaning to Afri         hant statistics. Twelve feet high at the shoulder r         ican bull's head is level with an eighteen-whe         ailer; seven tons of power means he can dera         motive. His 500-pound trunk can pick you         oll, and squash you like a rotten avocado         Or he can push over that tree you though         ape up. His smaller cousin with the small         an elephant, is nine-and-a-half feet tall and         e tons—a mere lightweight compared to the w         ull elephant.

for all their great size, elephants can walk into         h no warning. Their great padded feet are like         nd often the only warning of the presence of ele-         at night is the overpowering, circus-lot smell of urine.         nly sound may be the rumbling of the elephants' stom-         —which is really a means of communication elephants         when separated by thick bush. When they sense danger,         ey can stop the stomach rumblings at will.

The ghostlike stealth of an elephant can be attested to by a friend of Jack's and mine who spent one terrifying night camping in the bush. Since it had been an exceptionally hot night, the young man decided to make his bed on top of his Land Rover rather than pitch his tent. His companion decided to sleep in his own tent. Once the young man became comfortable on the Land Rover roof rack, he soon fell asleep. Hours later, he was awakened when he felt the Land Rover move slightly. He was annoyed, thinking his friend was searching for some item in the luggage. Then he felt something drop with a thud on the roof rack, and something touch his leg. Now angry, he was just about to swear at his friend for disturbing his sleep when he opened his eyes and saw a huge black form outlined against the moonlight. Frozen with fear, he was eyeball to eyeball with an elephant! The tip of the tusker's trunk was now touching his pants legs as the elephant felt around for food. By luck, the man had stored all the fruit and vegetables inside the vehicle before he retired. There was no way he could warn his friend in the tent. The minutes dragged on like hours as the elephant's trunk continued to probe around the luggage on the roof. Satisfied that there were no goodies on the rack, the elephant withdrew its trunk, and then turned and walked silently out of camp. The man nearly had a heart attack, while his friend snored away, oblivious to the seven-ton visitor.

There have been many heart-stopping incidents where campers in Amboseli have been caught unaware by elephants. Several years ago, a herd of fifteen or so entered a campsite where three families from Nairobi were making preparations for cooking. Luckily, the families had not yet removed the food from the Land Rovers parked some distance away. The people were so busy trying to get the campfire going for breakfast that they did not see the elephants until they were 75 feet away, shuffling along directly toward them. Frantically, the parents scooped up their small children, and since the vehicles were too far away, raced directly into one large tent and zipped up all the flaps. An eternity went by as the parents heard the crashing of camp equipment. Then the campsite became silent. One mother later recalled the awful stillness, listening for the slightest noise, holding onto her children, the terror intensified because they could not see what the elephants were up to. Then, slowly, several huge shadows began to creep up the walls, completely surrounding and darkening the tent. A zoo-stall animal smell was now overwhelming. All they could do was wait and try to control their mounting terror nearing panic. To have tried making a bolt for it out of the tent would have been certain suicide. Then black outlines of trunks began snaking up and down the tent walls like giant vacuum hoses. Smelling no food inside the tent, the elephants lost interest, the shadows receded and the tent lightened as the elephants moseyed off. If food had been left inside the tent, those families would have had a fatal pressing engagement with the pachyderms.

Sitting out there under the stars, we all felt a little more vulnerable when we heard the elephant trumpet again. We had spooked ourselves talking about the elephant camp encounters. When we retired to our tents for the night, I regretted having pitched my tent a little way from the trees. As I lay awake for awhile listening to the cricket symphony, I started to think about elephant statistics again. Elephants have feet and legs the size of tree trunks. It seemed to me that my tent was getting much smaller.

The next morning Jack, Elaine, and I had all gotten up an hour before daybreak to make breakfast earlier than usual. We wanted to take pictures of Kilimanjaro at sunrise. I had just added wood to the campfire when I heard Elaine whisper, "I think we have visitors." I looked around in the dark, but could see nothing. But when I focused, I could just make out several black forms, about 100 feet away, next to the acacias. Elephants had quietly moved out from the swamp in the night, and were now congregating in great numbers around the campsite. Their nearness was alarming.

Certainly the elephants heard our stirrings about, but they remained uninterested in our doings as they began to tear off branches and strip leaves off the acacias. Our only concern was that they might move toward the tents where our companions were still snoring away. As Jack and Elaine began to put the food back in the van, I silently rushed over to the tents to arouse my friends. They zipped out of their sleeping bags in a flash when I mentioned that elephants are not always polite enough to step over tents.

As we all stood watching near the campfire, we counted

some twenty-four elephants. Some of the tuskers had now decided to move off and we watched their black forms ambling onto the open sandy ground. Soon the rest of the herd left the acacias and, in single file, shuffled across the sands like a giant caravan.

As we had coffee and breakfast by the campfire, Jack and I reminded the others that though elephants are basically peaceful animals, no two elephants are alike. Some are unflappable, while others are simply "touchy" in the presence of man. Jack and I were aware of the risks of wandering around outside the campsite. In the bush, wild animals are not so much to be feared as to be respected—since they are always unpredictable. Jack and I had never been interested in courting danger in order to regale listeners with embellished "chest-thumping" stories, or the obligatory hairbreadth escapes around every turn in the path. But danger can arise from carelessness—and this was to be one of those days.

As the sky lightened, we noticed that Kilimanjaro was still cloud-free, and decided to walk out onto the sandy clearing some distance from camp to take photos. Elaine decided to stay in camp to tidy up her kitchen. The elephants seemed to have moved far off from the area.

After finishing our breakfast, we grabbed our cameras and headed out onto the clearing. As we moved to about 700 feet away from the camp, we all started to look through our viewfinders, getting shots of Kilimanjaro as it changed colors in the spectacular sunrise.

We had become so absorbed with our cameras that we had completely forgotten to keep our eyes open for elephants. But when I put my camera down to reload the film, I noticed two elephants emerging from a copse of acacias about 400 feet away in front of us. They were shuffling along in profile within line of the mountain, a perfect camera shot. The elephants seemed uninterested as they shambled along, stopping every so often to entwine their trunks around isolated clumps of grass, tearing it out by the roots, and then fastidiously shaking the dirt off against their knees, and delicately placing the morsels in their mouths like proper old English gentlemen at table. The elephants were the epitome now of serenity and good manners.

I alerted the others, but since the elephants were 400 feet away and were showing no interest in us, we went back to our camera business. As the mountain became pinkish, we were absorbed looking through viewfinders once again. What we didn't realize at the time was that one of the elephants had changed direction and had ambled straight toward us, and was watching our movements. He was now only 200 feet in front of us. I looked anxiously back at the camp and realized we had foolishly drifted two football field lengths from the campsite. I could just make out the small figure of Elaine bending over the campfire. When I looked back at the elephant, I realized he was taking an alarming interest in us as he quickened his pace a bit, his head swinging rhythmically from side to side, his ears flapping and snapping back and forth like stiff sheets in the wind. I warned the others, who were now stunned to see how close the elephant was, walking our way.

The elephant stopped again, lifted his head straight up, looked down over his upthrust tusks and unfurled his giant ears as big as the *Pinta* and the *Santa Maria*.

"Don't make any sudden moves!" Jack exclaimed as we all stood frozen in our tracks. "Certainly," we said, trying to find courage, "the elephant will stop. Certainly he is not interested in us."

But the elephant started up his slow pace, steadily shortening the distance between him and us. Slowly, we started to walk backwards, like linebackers anticipating the kick of the football. The elephant was now about 170 feet from us, taking wider strides, ears spread, his great yellow tusks held high. Then he stopped again and held his trunk up, getting our scent.

Aya was nervously urging us to run. I tried to calm her,

telling her that this was not the time to run. We still had a football field-and-a-half of ground to cover to get back to camp. Now movie images of tiny five-foot Osa Johnson standing her ground against a charging elephant flashed across my mind, but Osa had one advantage: a rifle. Professional hunters advise you to stand your ground, scream loudly, wave your arms above your head, but *don't* run. The screaming part would come easy for us as this Devout Coward Club continued to backpedal across the sands like a drill team in reverse. "Don't run! Don't run!" I kept trying to keep Aya from panicking, as the elephant now started to pace close to within 150 feet.

We looked around hopelessly for trees to climb, but there was nothing but sand and sparse clumps of grass. Suddenly, the elephant let loose a sky-shattering trumpet, lowered his head, ears pinned flat against his head, trunk curled against his chest, and began to start the chase. I turned to Aya who was screaming and shouted: "This is the time to run!"

Instantly, we all spun round on galvanized heels and began galloping across the sands bunched together like horses sprung from the gate at the Kentucky Derby, catapulted into the 100-yard dash back to camp. Luckily, we had a head start, but a parting glance over my shoulder showed the elephant quickly gaining speed. It was a paralyzing, helpless feeling, as though trapped on a trestle as a freight train comes pounding behind you at full throttle. We were stampeding straight for the trees at campsite, the elephant now padding silently behind us, kicking up puffs of dust in that singular rhythmic lumbering of a running elephant. Our feet did not seem to touch the ground as the elephant narrowed the gap to about 75 feet and in hot pursuit. My lungs felt like they would explode, adrenaline giving that extra push, eyes glued to the safety of the vehicles in the campsite. Aya and Ulla were now screaming as the elephant was 50 feet behind us and coming at great speed. When the elephant loomed 30 feet behind us, we came tearing through the acacias and raced to the Land Rover, dove in through the open doors, slammed them shut, and waited for that split second of impact. But the elephant had suddenly stopped in an explosion of dust by the trees, his head tossing back and forth, trumpeting indescribable, piercing, bloodcurdling screeches, then booming to low rumbling noises. His ears were flapping back and forth like giant semaphores, his trunk thrashing up and down in a fit of a bad temper tantrum, lost in clouds of dust. As he started to move back onto the open plains in a rage—I don't know what possessed me—I jumped out of the Land Rover and quickly snapped a picture of the elephant about 75 feet away, with his trunk up, trumpeting, his body backlit by the dust in the early morning light. Miraculously, during the chase, I had subconsciously clutched my camera in a death grip.

"Hey! Where's Elaine?" Brian and Pete shouted from the Rover's back seat. Just then, we heard the creaking of the van door behind us. When we looked back, a mop of orange hair emerged from the van door as Elaine peered nervously about, bug-eyed.

"Is it safe to come out now?" Elaine asked, visibly shaken from all the excitement. "When that elephant began to take an interest in you, I thought discretion the better part of valor and opened the Land Rover's doors. Then I hid in the van. There was nothing I could do . . . except take notes for your obituaries," she joked.

Then we all blurted out laughing like loons from our pent-up fear and adrenaline.

We were lucky. Jack and I blamed ourselves for being so stupid as to put our friends in jeopardy with one careless moment. I expressed the unpopular idea at the moment that elephants are basically peaceful animals, and that this old tusker probably was in a feisty, party mood and wanted to have a little fun with us.

"Oh, sure," Aya snapped. "A festive mood, like at the Mardi Gras—the elephant playing with his human piñatas."

As we tried to calm ourselves down, someone suddenly remembered the cameras and the tripods. I picked up my binoculars and focused in on the sandy plain in front of us. I was amazed to see the cameras and tripods still standing in their upright positions where we had abandoned them to the elephant.

Leaving the others behind in camp, Jack and I drove the Rover out onto the open sandy area. Fortunately the elephant had moved off to rejoin his companions in the brush. About halfway across the open, I noticed something sticking up out of the sand. Jack stopped the Rover, and I climbed out to have a look. As I walked closer to the two black objects sticking up, it dawned on me what I was seeing. I immediately doubled over with laughter. Jack could not figure what had happened, most likely wondering if I had snapped. The two objects in the sand were the sandals that belonged to Aya. They had not just been carelessly abandoned on the ground. Each sandal was dug into the sand toe first, the heels sticking straight up in the air—poised in a running position that launched Aya across the sands with the elephant hot on our heels.

Deciding we'd had enough of elephants for awhile, we soon picked up our stakes and headed easterly for Tsavo National Park. We planned to spend the night on a dirt track off the main Nairobi-Mombasa road, since we wanted to be on the Kenya coast the following morning.

Several hours after we'd left Amboseli, we drove through a landscape that could have been on the red planet Mars. The iron soil of Tsavo had painted everything red-orange: the nineteen-foot-high termite mounds, and the trees alongside the road. Even the great herds of elephants were orange from their many dust baths. Our skin was red from the dust blowing in the windows, and when we removed our sunglasses, we noticed we looked like red raccoons. Huge, potbellied trees, known as the African baobab, were as big around as two Kansas grain silos. Yet the baobab's branches were puny and spindly compared to the girth of the trunk. Since those branches look more like a network of roots, the Africans aptly named the baobab the "upside-down tree."

Orange elephant herds were everywhere—alongside the road, and in great numbers by water holes. After Amboseli, I noticed there was a distinct lack of interest in seeing elephants up close.

That evening, when we chose a campsite off the main Nairobi-Mombasa road, I noticed Aya was not wearing her sandals. She had evidently chosen to wear sneakers, her "fast get-a-way" shoes just in case any other elephants had ideas for a pachyderm marathon.

# 9

I T WAS 5:00 A.M. and pitch-black when we repacked all camping gear, and then followed our headlamps back down the little bush track and turned onto the Nairobi-Mombasa road. In this area, the main road divides Tsavo East from Tsavo West National Park, and we'd have to drive slowly and keep our eyes peeled for the possibility of herds of elephants, giraffes, or other animals straying across the road. Night driving is risky, since one often does not see the black forms of animals, even elephants, in the reflection of head lamps until it is too late. As night traffic has increased between Nairobi and Mombasa recently, there have been many gory accidents when speed-crazy drivers have been killed in head-on confrontations with elephants.

A couple of hours later as a sulphur light crept up the horizon, we were less than an hour from Mombasa. The dry bush, or *nyika* country, began to turn sticky and humid as we got closer to the coast. Gradually, we were leaving the vast brown landscape behind and entering a green world of coconut palms, banana *shambas*, and stands of mango and papaya trees. Little palm-thatched huts became more evident as the vegetation turned more lush.

As soon as the sun was up, we were in high spirits with visions of waving palm trees, cool ocean breezes, wide white beaches, and turquoise waters.

"The first thing I'm going to do when we camp on the deserted beach north of Malindi town tonight is prepare the best lobster dinner you've ever had," Elaine said.

Before long, we found ourselves in the flowing morning traffic as we crossed the Macupa Causeway taking us directly into Mombasa town. To our right, in the modern harbor, were fleets of cargo ships from all over the world. Mombasa is actually on an island connected to the mainland by the Causeway. A ferry boat service connects Mombasa to the south beaches and the Nyali Bridge ties it to the north coast.

The humid, sticky atmosphere, even in the morning, clings to you like a rubber suit. As soon as we drove onto Mombasa's tree-lined main boulevards, we were suddenly transformed into another world of Kenya culture. Mombasa is a fascinating hodgepodge of white-washed shops, old colonial hotels, Hindu temples, Muslim mosques, curry restaurants, tourist offices, supermarkets, and donkey carts that sometimes stop the flow of car and truck traffic. The New Town, which offers the amenities of any modern city, has grown up around Mombasa's Old Town. But the Old Town is Middle Eastern in flavor with its web of narrow alleyways, continuously connected houses with overhanging balconies, towers and minarets of temples and mosques far above the rusting tin roofs of the town.

Jack and I wanted our companions to taste this life by walking through the old section. While Jack stayed with the vehicles on one of the main streets, I guided my companions toward the Old Town, which you suddenly enter by taking a short diversion off a main thoroughfare. The narrow alleyways and recessed doorways on houses with louvered windows appear as an exotic scene from an oriental movie. The Swahili men we passed in the alleys wore ankle-length robes called *khanzus*, and the Arab men wore colorful beaded hats and embroidered cloth robes. The Asian women were bedecked in dazzling bright saris or punjabi trousers. The only drab dressers were the Muslim women, in their long head-to-toe black *buibuis*, their faces hidden by black veils. (Elaine wondered why they didn't faint flat out in the heat.)

This conglomerate of African, Asian, and Arab peoples reflects the diversity of life on Kenya's coast. The people of mixed Arab and African Bantu origin may be broadly termed as Swahilis. They speak the mulatto language, Swahili, which is of mixed Bantu and Arabic origin. Nearly ten centuries ago, when sea traders from Arabia first settled along the coast, they intermarried with the African inhabitants. Their descendents became known as the Swahili, based on the Arabic word *suahil*, which means "coastland."

The Swahili shopkeepers were just then opening their shops for business. The stuffy, tiny, dingy shops were all squeezed together and were nothing more than "hole-in-the-wall" establishments. Goldsmiths, silversmiths, tailors, and sweet meat sellers beckoned us to enter. The alleyways reeked of smells of dried fish, curry, cinnamon, and baking unleavened bread. Perfume shops wafted scents of jasmine and frangipani. We decided to enter one little dark shop for breakfast. Once we ignored the flies, we munched on the crunchy, triangular-shaped, hot-spiced pies called *samosas*. We washed these down with bitter, strong Turkish coffee served from copper pots called samovars. The coffee was thick enough to do a lube job on the Land Rover.

After breakfast, Elaine stopped in one of the spice shops and bought curry powder, cinnamon, sesame seeds, cayenne pepper, mango chutney, anise seeds, and Heaven knows what else she planned for her "Arabian Nights" dinner on the beach. She struck up a lively conversation with a friendly Indian shopkeeper, and it wasn't too long before she was wangling an old family curry recipe out of the proprietor. The recipe probably dated back to the times when East Indians traded along the coast 900 years ago. But no matter, Elaine would adopt the recipe as her very own.

At the end of one alleyway, the bleached dome of the Jain

Temple looked like white icing on a giant wedding cake. The towers and minarets of temples and mosques throughout the Old Town reflect the influence of the Hindu and Muslim religions. The Arab traders introduced the Muslim religion on the coast about 100 years after the death of the prophet Muhammed.

We were now sweating buckets, and decided to return to the vehicles to move on to the cooler air of the ocean. When we got back to the vehicles, we noticed that Jack, sitting in the Land Rover, looked as though he had been hosed down by the fire department. Before Jack melted completely, we piled back into the vehicles and threaded our way through the morning traffic.

A short while later we crossed the Nyali Bridge, and off to our right was a grand view of Mombasa's Old Harbour and the Old Town with its white-faced houses and red tin roofs.

Long before we spotted the Indian Ocean, the intoxicating ambrosia of salty sea air had our spirits soaring. "I've never seen a gloomy person on a sandy beach yet!" Elaine laughed as we turned onto the road toward Malindi town. To our right, many of the older one-story, tile-roofed, colonial-style hotels are found along the north coast, tucked back into palm groves and tangled vegetation.

Then the sweep of the Indian Ocean was revealed between a grove of palms. Having been landlocked for many days, the sudden appearance of the blue-green ocean beckoned us to turn off the main road onto a sandy track, past the palms, up to the old Coraldene Beach Cottages. We stepped out of the vehicles, tossed off our shoes, walked onto the white sands, and waded into the water. Here there is no surf, only the constant roar of the water as it breaks over the fringing coral reef several hundred yards from shore. As far as we could see there were miles of sandy beaches and waving palms. You feel as though you could build a little grass shack and stay here for the rest of your life. But there is an old colonial saying that warns of the dangers of living on the coast: "The first week you gets to the coast, you just sits and thinks. After the second week, you just sits!"

Heeding the advice, we got back into the vehicles for the two hour or so ride to Malindi. About halfway there we reached the Kilifi Creek where cars must cross by using a small ferry boat. Since there has been little tourism north of Mombasa until recently, no one had ever seen the need for a bridge. We liked it that way, the snail's pace of the coast—the best cure from ulcers in the world.

We passed many *makuti* (palm-thatched) huts clustered under coconut groves. The coconut sellers at little fruit stands waved us down. We couldn't resist and pulled over. At once, several African men chopped the tops off the coconuts with their *pangas* (machetes), and then we drank the milk straight from these football-size coconuts. It was the most refreshing beverage we'd had on safari and cost only five cents.

Remarkably, the coconut palm is not indigenous to Africa, but was introduced by Indonesian traders centuries ago. Now coconut palms proliferate all along the African coast. The coastal people use the coconut for just about everything: fronds for matting and thatching, and fibers for ropes and boat rigging. They even make a palm wine from the tree.

Elaine bought a box of coconuts, big juicy limes, oranges, bananas, pawpaws (papaya), passion fruit, and a bag of cashews. Elaine had some idea for a recipe up her sleeve for Far Eastern food. It was appropriate since it was the Arab and Asian traders who introduced mangoes, bananas, limes, lemons, and oranges to Africa. (The Portuguese traders, in the 1500s, introduced casavas, maize, tomatoes, and tobacco from the Americas.)

An hour later, we reached Watamu village, not far from Malindi, and turned down a sandy track past tangled vegetation and palms heading straight for beautiful Turtle Bay. This area is now a Marine National Park where no one can disturb the reef fish life, or take colorful seashells for souvenirs.

When the beach came into view, a strong ocean breeze cooled us as we pulled up to the sleepy, Seafarers Cottages that are but a few steps from the water. The blue-green waters and bleached beaches were blinding in the searing midafternoon sun. To the left of the Bay, dead coral reefs made a small lagoon a hundred yards from the white foam wall of the reef.

It was here at Watamu, back in the 1950s, that Joy and George Adamson brought their lioness, Elsa, to play on the beach and swim in the Indian Ocean. In 1964, Columbia Pictures recreated the Elsa swim scene at this very site, using movie lions who alternately portrayed Elsa.

At the Seafarers, we rented our goggling gear of swim masks, flippers, and snorkels. Since it was low tide, the owners of the cottages provided a small boat with an African guide to take us near the reef.

"You can include me in on this adventure," Elaine exclaimed. "Beaches are my thing, and I was a champion swimmer at the YWCA."

Changing into our swimsuits, we waded out several hundred feet to waist-deep water, wearing tennis shoes to avoid stepping on sharp coral, barnacles, and the pincushion stabbing spines of sea urchins. Then we climbed into the little *mtumbwi* (canoe) as two Africans paddled us out to the reef.

Since the Bay was calm, we could peer straight down into the crystal-clear water to observe the different species of coral. Large schools of outrageously colored reef fish swarmed around the canoe. When we got closer to the foaming water, roaring over the reef, the Africans then pointed down to a coral shelf from where we could begin snorkeling. We should have brought T-shirts to prevent sunburn from the blazing equatorial sun. But we were too lazy to turn back—a decision we would later regret.

When we got to the coral shelf, we put on our flippers and waited for one African, carrying a spear gun as a precaution, to guide us down among the reefs. The other African would stay with the canoe.

"What about sharks?" Aya and Ulla asked, looking around apprehensively. Our guide reassured them that there are no sharks inside the barrier reef, but he did warn us to keep our eyes open for the scorpion fish whose long spines can inject a lethal poison.

The African told us to stick together and then, putting on our masks, we dove in after him. The shelf dropped off alarmingly and we were forced to swim, face masks down into the water as we floated along on top. Diving down several feet, we were in another dimension. The water was so clear that it was like a dustless vacuum, and there was no sensation of being underwater. My companions swimming alongside me seemed to be suspended in air. Almost instantly, several schools of reef fish began to gather around us. For a moment it was a bit unsettling to be among a wall of fish, but they are harmless, looking for handouts the guides sometimes bring with them.

These fish are dazzling, as though designed by free imaginations of kindergartners gone wild with phosphorescent paints. Each species of fish seemed to try to outshine the magnificence of the others. Some were brilliantly striped, while others were arrayed with rainbow colors, checkerboards, red masks, arabesque designs, and flashing colors that glitter in shafts of sun. Most of the fish are laterally flattened, so that when they face you head-on, they look like they had been squeezed through a pasta ringer. This flatness allows them to swim between the seaweed and the coral skeletons. It's a kaleidoscope world of sea life against the coral pink reefs. The reefs themselves are made up of coral polyps, actually living colonial animals distantly related to sea anemones. Each polyp secretes calcium carbonate to create a lime skeleton, which is connected to colonies of many thousands. The corals continuously build on their skeletons, growing upward and creating the "fringing" reefs along the East African coast.

Diving deeper, our guide pointed out the brilliant starfish that look as if they were laced with red or blue icing; once exposed to the air, their colors fade. The African guide pointed down to the colorful mollusk shells appearing like fine hand-painted porcelain. Unfortunately, years ago, mollusk shells were carted away by the boxful by greedy tourists. To stop this plundering, the reef was declared a national park.

We were continually resurfacing for air and then diving again to see small octopuses, clams, and giant crayfish. The guide pointed upward to return to the surface when he spotted the flowing feathery array of the venomous, red spines of the scorpion fish only fifteen feet below us. We had become so absorbed in discovering more spectacular sea life that we had lost all track of time. Once on the surface again, the guide told us it was now 5:00 P.M. and that we should return to shore. Reluctantly, we swam to the coral shelf and climbed back into the canoe. Reaching the shallows, we jumped out of the canoe and waded to shore. We noticed that our skin was turning the color of boiled lobsters, noses turning clown red, lips cracking like bad plaster, and our shoulders blow-torched raw and pink. When we got back to the vehicles, we could barely stand to put on lotion. We were also parched, and headed into the tiny Seafarers bar for Tusker beers.

Our time was getting short, since we wanted to stop at the Malindi fish market before heading on north to the deserted beach. We hoped to set up camp before sunset. When we climbed into the vehicles, we all howled and yelped like coyote pups when our sunburnt bodies made contact with the hot seats.

Half an hour later we pulled into the sleepy seaside town of Malindi. Decades ago, Hemingway went deep-sea fishing here and stayed at the Blue Marlin, which was then the only hotel in town. We arrived at the little fish market, where

Elaine picked out the biggest live lobsters and giant crabs she could find. Then we were off across a dirt road heading north.

It took another hour and a half until we found a little track that diverted east off the main road. The sun was just about going down when we reached a small embankment that overlooked the spectacular sweep of beach of Formosa Bay. Because fresh water from the Tana River, north of us, flows into the ocean for some distance, the reef ends not far from Malindi. Coral cannot survive when in contact with fresh water.

Because there was no fringing reef at Formosa Bay, there were miles and miles of pounding surf to our left and right. There wasn't a human species in sight. Behind the flat expanse of sand were large windblown dunes covered with sparse vegetation and the slim casuarina trees with their feathery-leafed branches. We did not set up our tents, since we wanted to sleep under the stars. We found a low rise just behind the sand dunes to park the vehicles.

It was now dark, and we turned on our camp floodlights to begin setting up the safari kitchen. We poured water from the jerry cans into three huge pots for boiling the lobsters and crabs on the stoves. Jack and I carried the dining table onto the top of a small sand dune overlooking the beach. While Aya and Ulla began cutting up the fruit for the salad, Brian and Pete set the giant crabs and lobster next to Elaine at her worktable. Although the East African lobster is actually a large crayfish with no pincers, the giant crabs had claws large enough to snip off thumbs. Luckily, their claws were tied shut with wires. Once the table was set, we were ready to boil the lobsters.

"You'll have to be the ones to drop the lobsters and crabs into the boiling water," Elaine said seriously to Jack. "I hate killing anything."

"I get to be the executioner, I see," grumped Jack. "Your conscience won't be bothering you, though, once you start smothering them in parsley butter."

"Oh, no," Elaine said, as we heard the lobsters and crabs plop into the water. "I can't watch."

"Relax, Elaine," Jack drolled. "I gave them their last rites."

Before long, we were sitting at the table set with bright Coleman pressure lamps. The red, steaming lobsters were on platters in front of us, as well as fruit salad and garlic bread. "Crack, crack, crack" was the only sound as we broke open the lobster shells and crab claws, and then dipped the huge pink-white morsels into the melted butter. We were so absorbed with these delicacies that we didn't talk.

After dinner, we turned off the pressure lamps, and gazed up into the stars. The only sound was the rhythmic pounding of the surf, and the soft rustling of the casaurina trees. Here on the deserted beach one can imagine what the entire East African coast looked like when the Arab and Asian traders first sailed here some 2,000 years ago. Through those centuries, old sailing ships called *dhows* from Arabia and the Far East rode the northeast monsoons from December to March. The *dhows* carried spices, glass, ironware, wheat, and wine. Then, from April to November, the *dhows* returned on the southeast monsoons carrying rhino horns, tortoise shells, ivory, and slaves from Africa. In the Middle Ages, great trading towns with sultans' palaces, mosques, and houses squeezed together along narrow streets sprouted along the coast. But internal strife, caused by feuding trading towns, gradually destroyed the cities, which fell into decay. Today, only crumbling ruins remain of such towns as Pate, Manda, and Gedi. One place of great mystery, where the mystique of the Arabian Nights still exists, frozen in time, is a place called Lamu. In a day's time, we would return to the Middle Ages to explore this living fossil.

Much later, while finishing up our dinner dishes, we noticed the rising of the half-moon above the horizon. We decided to take a moonlight swim in the surf.

"My God! The beach is moving!" Elaine blurted out.

Like something out of science fiction, we saw thousands of tiny dark shapes crawling across the sand. Little ghost crabs covered the beach like a carpet, scuttling in and out of their sand burrows, and running in and out of the edges of the waves. Since they dislike the hot sun, they come out on moonlit nights. Hence their name: "ghost crabs."

As we scattered crabs out of the way, many began to seek the safety of their burrows. They are harmless critters, but would probably drive a dog bonkers.

As our toes dug into the sandy ocean bottom, we stumbled our way through the surf, to swim and ride the waves. With the half-moon reflected in the water, I was reminded of a true story told by an old hunter years ago. North of the Tana River there are large herds of elephants that live in swamps near the ocean. The hunter told of camping on the beach one night near a swamp. Awakening in the moonlight, he had to rub his eyes to make certain what he was seeing in the ocean was real. A herd of elephants had emerged from the swamp and was wading chest-high in the breakers, their tusks glowing in the moonlight.

As we swam in the moonlight, I told everyone to take a long, hard look, since international developers are planning to build high-rise hotels and condos on Formosa Bay. Already, near Mombasa, some of the older colonial-style hotels are being torn down for high-rise, high-priced tourist hotels.

Elaine was disturbed by this. "How ironic," she said. "The Elite of the world, and the developers, will spend huge sums of money to live here in the future, having destroyed the very solace and beauty they wanted to have in the first place."

Here we were seeing it before the crowd arrived. Seeing it untouched, and leaving it untouched. Who are the rich ones?

# 10

Stretched out on top of my sleeping bag on the beach, I awakened at dawn, opened my eyes and stared straight into the face of a ghost crab. His pincers raised, he meant business guarding his burrow, squaring off for a knockdown, drag-'em-out fight. Since he had thousands of pugilist pals, I decided discretion was the better part of valor.

The dawn bloomed pink across the horizon reflecting on the sea. I roused my companions and told them we wanted to be on the road to reach Lamu Island by afternoon. After a light breakfast and then repacking our gear, we were back on the dirt road heading north toward the Tana River. At the little shack town of Garsen, a small ferry boat took our vehicles and us across the Tana, Kenya's largest river whose source is the Aberdare Mountains several hundred miles to the west.

It was a primitive road as we headed toward Witu town, but we blessed this horrible track since it has mainly kept large numbers of tourists away. A new airstrip on the mainland across from Lamu Island is beginning to bring in the "jet set" who stay at the Shela Beach Hotel on the island.

A few hours later, we reached Mokowe village. Since no vehicles are permitted on Lamu Island, it was necessary to leave our vehicles near a small police station in town for safekeeping. After organizing a few clothes in knapsacks for an overnight stay in Lamu, we walked to the boat dock which faces Lamu town.

I had talked a lot about the charm of Lamu, but my companions were not prepared for the sudden appearance of a storybook town. Several hundred yards across the bay from the dock stood a long line of dilapidated, double-balconied houses that were scrunched up together on the long promenade facing the mainland.

When we climbed down into the motor launch with several Africans, we were off on the short ferry trip across the bay. Reaching the jetty, we docked close to several *dhows* which had sailed in from Arabia on the northeast monsoon. Lamu men, in their long white *khanzus* and Muslim hats, were loading the sailing ships with mangrove poles (used for building houses) to ship to Arabia where there are no trees for lumber.

At the jetty, we climbed steep cement steps up the seawall to the promenade. In front of the double-balconied, white coral-rag houses, the promenade was vibrant with life. Swahili men crying, "Buy my limes!" led donkeys that were laden with huge burlap bags of limes. Whiffs of curry and dried fish hung heavily on the salty air. A few Muslim women in their black *buibuis* slipped between the shadows of the houses. The old *dhows* creaked and groaned in the soft breeze of the blue bay. It was a living page from the *Arabian Nights* and Sinbad the Sailor. Although those tales, written centuries ago in Baghdad were of course fiction, Sinbad's ports of call were based on the real towns of the East African coast.

"I don't think we're in Kansas anymore, Toto," Elaine said as we tried to comprehend our sudden transformation back to Sinbad's world.

Since it was now late afternoon, we wanted to find lodging for the night. We took a walk behind the promenade houses and entered the Old Town section. We found ourselves within a confusing maze of alleyways made up of walls of continuously connected two- and three-story houses. These alleys were barely a yard wide, and we often had to step aside into alcoves to let Lamu men pass by, leading their donkeys in single file. Legend has it that these streets had been made narrow and twisting so as to prevent invading armies from sacking the town. These constricting passageways blocked out the sun, and we lost our sense of direction.

"Didn't we just walk down this same alley before?" Aya stood perplexed.

"Why don't we try this one to the right," Pete said.

Turning down one tunnel, we suddenly walked into blinding sunlight of an oriental flower garden surrounding a palm-shaded, crumbling double-balcony house. It had, like many of the larger houses, the two-piece Lamu doors set within intricately carved doorframes.

After being lost for awhile, we finally found a guest hostel down one of the alleys. A small sign on the door read: "Knock for Hotel Manager." We banged the knocker, and slowly the door creaked open to reveal a huge, portly man wearing a turban. When we inquired about lodging, he invited us in to the dark, cool reception room. The house looked like a cave house with rounded white ceilings and oval-shaped rooms; Persian carpets lay on the floors, and large overstuffed cushions were used as seats.

After we checked in, the proprietor asked us to follow him up a steep flight of stairs to the upper two stories. Each tiny, cocoon-sized room had a canopy bed and a carved Zanzibar chest. The third floor had a balcony overlooking a labyrinth of alleys; a small garden below was shaded by tamarind trees.

As it was getting on to late afternoon, we decided to head off for a restaurant to sample the local food. The proprietor recommended the Petley Inn that overlooks the bay. The aged building was once the private home of a wealthy Arab family, and had only recently been converted into a hotel. Climbing two flights up an old staircase, we arrived at the open-air, rooftop restaurant that had a splendid view of the *dhow*

harbor. A heaven-sent breeze flapped the white linen tablecloths on the neatly set tables. The houses and mosques of
the Old Town created an illusion that nothing had changed
since the founding of Lamu in the seventh century, in which
it eventually became an international trading center in ivory
and slaves. Across the bay, we could see the wall of the
mangrove swamp where, even to this day, herds of elephants
are found—now the target of poachers for their ivory.

We decided to select from a wide variety of curry dishes
from the buffet table. The table was laden with spicy meats
and poultry, white rice, *chapatis* (unleavened bread), and all
kinds of fruit and coconuts. We heaped our plates with the
rice pilaf, seasoned with cloves, pepper, cinnamon, and gin-
ger. There were also entrees of roast mutton and shish kabobs,
bananas cooked in coconut milk, and fish cooked in spiced
yogurt. Some dishes are topped off with crushed coconut,
mango chutney, and cashew nuts.

As we savored our dinner, we watched the sun set behind
the mangrove swamp across the harbor. Within minutes,
streetlamps along the promenade and throughout the town
winked on.

When we returned down the dark streets to the guest house,
the proprietor gave us candles for our rooms. Our shadows
inflated, twisted, and wavered all along the walls and staircase
as we followed the flickering candles up to the balcony. Elaine
loved this, imagining an exotic locale of intrigue and jewel
smugglers.

As we sat on the balcony, enjoying the breeze and lights
of the Old Town, Jack and I told our companions that we
would leave early the following morning to begin our long
journey to the most exciting safari country in East Africa:
the Northern Frontier. We were partial to the Frontier's vast
open spaces, 125,000 square miles of black lava deserts,
mountains, palm-fringed rivers, and species of game not
found anywhere else in Kenya. When I mentioned Marsabit
mountain, and that we'd be camping for our first time at

Lake Paradise, Elaine practically jumped out of her chair.

"Lake Paradise!" Elaine exclaimed. "That's where Martin and Osa Johnson lived!"

"*You know* about Lake Paradise and the Johnsons?" I asked, surprised.

"Are you kidding?" Elaine said. "Remember, I'm a grandmother, for heaven's sake. I grew up on their documentary films and I read Osa's book, *Four Years in Paradise*, over and over. Back in the 1920s and '30s the Johnsons' films created a sensation because in those days, when movies were in their infancy, people had never before seen authentic films of African wild animals and primitive tribes in their natural environment—actually moving across the big screen. I remember standing in long lines at the theater and gawking up at the huge, gaudy canvas posters above the marquee that trumpeted the Johnsons' real-life adventures. The Johnsons made *safari* a household word. People worldwide adored the Johnsons, especially the glamorous Osa, who was one of the best-dressed women in the world. The Johnsons' films made them as popular as any movie stars of the day.

"But I best remember the Johnsons' home and film laboratory perched on top of the crater rim overlooking a spoon-shaped lake, and Marsabit forest veiled by Spanish moss and mist."

Elaine was excited that she'd be able to connect with her childhood dream, and her enthusiasm got everyone anticipating camping in Marsabit forest.

"After all these years," Elaine added, "I wonder what remains at Paradise of the Johnsons' old mud-brick house that had a veranda overlooking the crater lake, a bath, a bedroom, living room with fireplace, library, and a complete kitchen where Osa tried out her gourmet recipes. She also had a vegetable garden that was raided by an elephant they called Sweet Potato."

"We'll just have to do a little exploring on the crater rim once we get to Paradise," Jack said.

When we retired to our rooms, I think each one of us had a vision of Paradise and the magic we would experience.

The next morning I was awakened by a stir of activity down in the alleyway below my third-story window. I opened the louvered sash and peered down at several Swahili men leading their donkeys to the jetty.

Once we were all up and organized, we headed into town for breakfast at Petley's Inn to await the 9:00 A.M. ferry.

Later, when we had walked to the dock, we began the ferry boat ride back to the mainland. We took one last look back at the promenade of the old houses and the *dhows* in the harbor, hoping it would not all dissolve suddenly like some Arabian Brigadoon.

At Mokowe, we paid the African security man who had watched the vehicles, and began the long drive back down the coast. Hours later, we turned west onto a dirt track that eventually led into the Tsavo East National Park. Since we wanted to be in the Frontier in three days, we would camp for only one night in Tsavo. The following day we connected up with the main Mombasa road that took us to Nairobi by nightfall. We decided to stay one night at the Ainsworth Hotel so that the following day we could reprovision our supplies of meat, vegetables, and Dry Ice. Once we reached the Northern Frontier, we would find it impossible to get the food supplies we'd need.

On the third day after leaving the coast, we checked out of the Ainsworth and drove north out of Nairobi into the edge of Kenya's highlands. We planned to drive six hours straight to reach Buffalo Springs-Samburu Reserves in the Frontier before nightfall to set up camp.

An hour's drive north from Nairobi, we passed acres and acres of pineapple plantations near Thika and decided to have our one stop for lunch at the old Blue Posts Hotel that faces the 80-foot high Chania (Kikuyu for "noisy") Falls near Thika town. The Blue Posts was where pioneer farmers once outspanned their oxen and carts for a rest. The hotel was made famous by one of Kenya's premier English settlers, writer Elspeth Huxley, who wrote *The Flame Trees of Thika*.

From Thika we traveled into the rolling hill country where large coffee tree plantations stretch as far as the eye could see. These highlands that surround Mount Kenya are the traditional tribal lands of the Bantu-speaking Kikuyu, Kenya's largest tribe numbering nearly 3.5 million. First settling here over four centuries ago, the Kikuyu maintained an agricultural existence because of the highlands' rich soil. When the British colonists set up their own farms in the early 1900s, a confrontation between the British and the Kikuyu was inevitable. The conflict first erupted in 1952 when small bands of forest guerrilla fighters began attacking and terrorizing settlers' farms at the base of Mount Kenya and the Aberdare Mountains. Although the British eventually put down the uprising by terrorists who became known as Mau Mau, the African voices crying for freedom could no longer be ignored. It was a Kikuyu man who led his fellow Kenyans to independence from Great Britain in 1963. That man was Jomo Kenyatta, who became Kenya's first president.

Our vehicles continually changed gears as we rolled up the steep hills and down through the valleys. Hundreds of little huts, peppered across the patchwork of maize fields, puffed out little pencils of smoke spiraling up through the grass-roofed dwellings. Aromatic woodsmoke permeated the cold air.

Climbing a few thousand feet in elevation, we could see the ribbon of road snaking miles into the distance and rising toward the lower slopes of Mount Kenya, now cloaked with a mantle of clouds. We hoped to get a glimpse of the glacier peaks by late afternoon. Passing through the old colonial town of Nyeri, we remarked that the large English-style estates, with rolling lawns and neatly clipped hedges, looked more like the dales of England than Africa.

Soon after passing through Timau village, we climbed even

higher. To our left we found ourselves staring into the stark open space of the Timau escarpment.

"Will you look at that!" Aya shouted from the Land Rover's back seat. "We've got to stop and take a close look at this."

Pulling the vehicles over to the side of the road, we stepped out. The wheat fields had abruptly dropped away, revealing below a salmon-colored sea of thorn scrub of semiarid desert sweeping away to infinity. The flat expanse was punctuated by small hills, and by the huge squared-off, tabletop mountain block called Ol Doinyo Sabachi far off in the distance, shimmering through heat waves. The desert road was but a faint scratch on the dusty surface as it led down to Isiolo, a *duka* town whose tin roofs flashed in the sun like bits of mica. We had arrived at the doorstep of the Northern Frontier.

We were standing on the edge between two different worlds: the desert before us, the lush Mount Kenya highlands behind us. Gradually the mantle of clouds thinned out on Mount Kenya's black shoulders of forest and unveiled two ragged snow-capped peaks thrusting up to over 17,000 feet. It is a scene more of the Swiss Alps than of equatorial Africa.

The first European explorer to see Mount Kenya was Johann Ludwig Krapf who, in 1849, described the mountain as "two large horns or pillars rising over an enormous mountain, shining white with glacier." The Wakamba tribe called the black-and-white mountain *Ke 'Nyaa*, the word for the black-and-white plumage of the male ostrich. This is how Kenya got its name.

Continuing on our way, the road dropped quickly in elevation, and a half hour later we entered the one-street town of Isiolo, the gateway to the Frontier. The village was nothing but a few tin shacks, mud-cement *dukas*, and a Barclay's Bank in the shape of a pink Beau Geste fort. Some three miles west of town is a small hilltop house where Joy and George Adamson once lived for many years. This is also where they kept their lioness, Elsa, before releasing her back to the wilds of the Meru Game Reserve.

At the north end of Isiolo, it is necessary to check in with an official at the sentry gate before entering the semidesert country. When the gate was raised, our vehicles followed a gravel road for a mile, and then we abruptly bumped onto a white, dusty, teeth-rattling corrugated track that leads into a vast expanse of thorn scrub and umbrella-shaped acacia trees. We had entered the Northern Frontier.

# 11

IT WAS NOW THE DRY SEASON in the Frontier, and clouds of dust were churned up by the Land Rover, powdering the van behind with a fine white sheet from the limestone earth. Miles ahead on the straight white track, we could see the massive square face of Ol Doinyo Sabachi looming above the horizon. This giant rock face is the sentinel of the Northern Frontier, beckoning the adventurer to this wild land.

Along the side of the track, we passed people of the Somali tribe leading their camels to Isiolo. The men wear togas, or *kikois*, that look like red-and-white checkered tablecloths, while the women are elegant in their long colorful dresses. These tall, thin, Islamic people with fine aquiline features are of Eastern Cushitic descent. Camels are the preoccupation of these nomadic pastoralists who roam freely across the Kenya-Somalia border—which they defiantly disregard—into the northeastern section of the Frontier. The camel is the center of their existence, supplying them with milk, their main staple, and permitting the Somalis complete freedom to roam the deserts. Somalis are proud, fiercely independent, tough people who have often made war on other tribes of the north. It is said that a Somali man can walk forty miles in the desert on only one cup of water.

An hour later, we turned left off the main road to head down a sandy track entangled with wait-a-bit thorns and acacia scrub toward the Buffalo Springs-Samburu Reserves.

One thing you notice about this reserve is the pungent, spicy smell to the earth. When we reached the ranger's post to check in, we had only an hour left of daylight before reaching our campsite.

"Hey, Richard," Elaine turned to me. "Why don't we cool off and get a better view of Samburu by sitting on *top* of the Land Rover?"

Jack thought poorly of the idea, but Elaine wouldn't take no for an answer. Jack grumped, but stopped the Land Rover and warned: "If you insist on riding on top, you'd better duck when we pass under the acacias. I'm not backtracking to pluck your scalps off the thorn branches."

Stepping outside the vehicle, Elaine and I climbed the little steel ladder up to the roofrack. We made seats for ourselves on the rack by arranging piled-up soft sleeping bags and rolls of canvas. We tied ropes onto the front of the rack for makeshift reins on our iron horse.

"We're ready to rip!" I shouted, banging against the side of the Rover. We lurched into gear and were off, holding on tightly to the reins.

"You're crazy!" Brian and Pete yelled and waved from the van behind us.

What a sensation of unbridled freedom as we swayed along the Samburu track. Only a few miles from the ranger's post, we were delighted to see a herd of fifty or so Grevy's zebras crossing the main track. The Grevy's species—unlike the plump-looking Burchell's zebras with their thick bars of stripes—have thin, vertical pinstripes like a seersucker suit that radiate in the sunlight. Supposedly a zebra's stripes radiate with light waves on the horizon, making them invisible to predators from long distances. But, to our eyes, zebras stand out like sore thumbs.

We decided to camp near Buffalo Springs at a campsite known as Champagne Ridge. The name certainly does not fit an African camping site, but it was named by a movie crew of Metro-Goldwyn-Mayer that shot scenes here for the film *Mogambo* in 1952. The crew was known to indulge heavily in champagne after filming hours. We took pleasure in knowing that we'd bivouac under the same umbrella acacia trees where Clark Gable, Ava Gardner, and Grace Kelly once camped.

We chose a camping site along Champagne Ridge that had a grand view of Mount Kenya, its snow-capped peaks some fifty miles to the south.

In the dimming light, we unloaded the camping equipment under the trees, and then set up the tables, chairs, and the safari kitchen. "Who invited the baboons?" Elaine asked as we watched a troop of forty baboons a hundred feet away climbing up into the acacias to watch the show. They were obviously hoping for a few handouts. Baboons are becoming bolder in the reserves because a few dim-witted campers have tossed scraps of food to them. Now the baboons expect handouts. As amusing as it might be for taking photos of baboons fighting over tidbits, it is dangerous. A full-grown 100-pound male baboon can easily bite off your hand with his steel-trap jaws, and long, razor-sharp canine teeth. On a safari a few months back, Jack and I had lunch near Buffalo Springs when suddenly an aggressive male baboon dropped down from a tree above us and snatched our large carton of forty-eight eggs right out from under our noses. Instantly, I was up and chased after him with a large stick as the baboon screamed and dropped the carton, and broke every single last egg. Neither baboon nor man was the victor.

Elaine decided to have an "African Night" with a recipe she had found in an old African cookbook. A couple of hours later, we sat down to a candlelit dinner: chunks of chopped-up chicken mixed with ground peanuts, sweet potatoes, garlic, and onions flavored with coriander and *sim sim* (sesame seeds), banana chips fried in coconut oil, and polished off with fresh passion fruit juice.

And, of course, right on schedule, Elaine snapped her Johnny Mathis tapes into her cassette player. "Oh, noooo!"

we all groaned in mock exasperation when we heard Mathis sing for the hundredth time: "There is someone walking behind you . . . turn around, look at me."

Later that evening, Jack, Elaine, and I decided to put our sleeping bags out under the stars, a little distance from the campfire. We had a special reason to do so since the moon was waxing toward full. The others, though, were playing chicken inside their tents because we had earlier heard lions grunting off in the distance.

The stars of Samburu seemed even closer to the ground as we lay on top of our sleeping bags, staring up into the sky into what looked like trillions of stars. Writer Robert Ruark described the Northern Frontier nights as "velvety, almost furry sky that canopied so low you could have reached up and plucked a star to make a necklace for your lady love."

A while later, the moon began to roll up the horizon, and poured liquid silver across the landscape. Far to the south, the glaciers of Mount Kenya were scoured white in the moonlight.

It was well after midnight when we drifted off to sleep. But I was suddenly awakened by muffled grunts coming from the trees. I strained my ears to hear above the insects and stared into the shadows beyond the campfire. I then realized that it was the baboons grumping among themselves up in the trees. When I tried to get back to sleep, I heard something rustling in the van, and then the loud rattling of silverware. I got up to have a look around in the firelight, and saw Elaine coming back from the van with a large butcher knife.

"Elaine," I said. "It's only the baboons making that grunting noise. Go back to sleep."

"Yeah, well," Elaine said, peering around nervously. "I've heard these lions in the Frontier are tricky. They probably disguise their grunts to *sound* like baboons. I've got this knife just in case."

Just when I thought I might get back to sleep, I heard more gruntings that sounded like buffalo. I lifted my head from the pillow, and switched my flashlight around, and finally found the source of the disturbance: Elaine was snoring away loudly—and still clutching her butcher knife in a death grip.

The next morning at the crack of dawn, we were awakened by the ear-piercing twitterings of hundreds of busy weaver-birds flying in and out of their nests woven with grass that hung down like Christmas ornaments. Their nerve-wracking chirping was like hundreds of kiddie-cart wheels that needed greasing.

Just as I got out of my sleeping bag, I heard a loud yelp and saw Pete in front of his tent, hopping up and down on one leg holding his foot, doing a Slovenian polka with much enthusiasm. When I went over to see what was up, Pete was smashing a tiny scorpion with his shoe. Although it was only a small scorpion, the painful red-hot poker stab of its stinger punishes you for not shaking out your shoes before putting them on.

After everyone got organized, and we had our breakfast, I reminded them that this was again laundry day. Our clothes had already washed and rinsed themselves in our large plastic buckets that agitated along the roads. After wringing out our clothes, we hung them on a long line strung between two acacias without bothering with clothespins, since the hot desert wind would dry the laundry in minutes.

We then squeezed into the Land Rover for the short ride to Buffalo Springs for a swim. When we arrived at the swimming pool-size springs, we noticed several herds of zebras, oryxes, and reticulated giraffes (their markings are reticulated patterns) roaming across an open plain. Supposedly, this little pool was created by explosives by the British Army decades ago. They had also built a little stone wall around the six-foot deep pool to keep out the crocodiles. Surprisingly, years ago, a crocodile had found its way from the Uaso Nyiro River to take up residence at the pool. It was later shot when it attacked a small child.

After changing into our swimsuits, we dove off the wall into the cool water. The spring is always crystal clear since it is filtered through limestone. What a luxury it was to have our own pool in the middle of this dusty landscape where the *Mogambo* cast once took dips after a hot day in front of the Technicolor cameras.

After our swim, we headed back to camp to pack up our laundry and supplies in order to move on to Samburu Reserve. When we arrived back at the campsite, Brian suddenly yelled out, "Hey, where in the blazes is our laundry?" The clothesline was empty.

"*There's* the laundry!" Aya said, pointing to some distant trees. "And there's more laundry over there, and more clothes beyond those trees . . ." In our absence, the strong desert winds had cleanly lifted all the clothes off the line and scattered them hundreds of feet all over the plains. Some shirts had impaled themselves on wait-a-bit thorns, socks hung on thorn tree branches, slacks draped over bushes, while underwear flapped in the breeze on lower branches. Our laundry looked like an explosion at the laundromat. Tears of laughter were already leaking from Orange Blossom's eyes as she reached for a Kleenex.

We walked a few hundred feet outside the camp to retrieve our scattered clothes. Caterwauling like a tomcat chorus as wait-a-bit thorns stitched our flesh like sail needles, we tried to oh-so-gently pick our torn clothing from the bush like dismantling a bomb. Our fingers and hands were bleeding and raw like cotton pickers as we worked away with incredible concentration. An hour or so later, after finally extracting the last thread, we gathered up our shredded clothing. When we reached camp, we met up with another disaster: a large troop of opportunistic baboons had been having a jolly good time pilfering our goodies in our absence. After our encounter with the thorns, we were in no mood for any baboon buffoonery, and immediately dropped our laundry, picked up sticks, and tore after them like vengeful Apaches. Taken by surprise, the baboons freaked out in alarm, shrieking like a band of gypsies caught rifling through a department store, trying to grab as much loot as they could, tearing off for dear life. Several baboons had cabbages and tomatoes stuffed in their mouths as well as carrying loot under their arms. Baboon adults, teenagers, and babies were everywhere, rioting in panic, emerging from tents as others carried bunches of bananas from out of the van. They say disasters come in threes: One large male baboon had a grip on my tin teacup and went up a tree with it. I was sentimentally attached to that battered old safari cup, but wondered what in tarnation a baboon would do with it. "Maybe he's going to make banana daiquiris," Jack said as we looked around at the shambles of ripped-open bags of rice, banana peels, torn cereal boxes, and bits and pieces of vegetables and fruit. Several baboons were still up in the trees bloating themselves with stolen fruit, and gloating over their victory of the Raid on Champagne Ridge.

After cleaning up the mess, we repacked the vehicles, preparing to set up another campsite in Samburu Reserve, just across the Uaso Nyiro River from Buffalo Springs Reserve. We drove down a sandy track heading for the river. There is something special about Samburu and the Frontier with its sheer rock faces and pyramid-shaped hills overlooking the thorn desert—a mixture of umbrella-shaped acacias and savannah grass, all stitched together by a lush, green palm-fringed river that teems with crocs and hippos. It is a time warp where nomadic people lead their camels across deserts they share with elephants that miraculously survive, by sheer pluck, in this parched land. In the dry season, the desert sun fries everything to cinders. Yet, incredibly within only forty-eight hours after heavy rains, the scraggly bush country begins to turn emerald green, the desert air perfumed by the sweet scent of the African earth. This land is, as Robert Ruark wrote, "desert-wasted, forgotten by Allah and avoided by Shaitan [the Swahili word for Satan], awful, terrifying, enticing, ugly . . . *lovely* Northern Frontier."

When we reached the Uaso Nyiro [Masai for "brown river"], the vegetation became thicker and greener. The wide Uaso Nyiro is spectacular because you do not expect to see such a large river flowing through semidesert country. The Uaso is lined with a fringe of magnificent doum palms, a palm distinctive to this river, with its V-shaped spreading branches topped off with fan-shaped leaves. The doum palms rustled metallically in the wind all along the riverbanks.

When we stepped out of the vehicles, several large, green-mottled crocodiles splashed into the river and submerged. These aggressive crocs have always been a menace to the Africans living near the riverbanks. Several months earlier, a British road-building crew had been working on a bridge over the Uaso when they heard screams coming from below. When they looked over the bridge, the men were horrified to see a small African boy being dragged into the water by a croc. They immediately raced down to the bank, brandishing hammers and wrenches, anything to hit the croc with. But by the time they reached the bank, the croc was swimming out in midstream, holding the small limp figure of the boy between its jaws. It is an ugly reminder that, even though everything can look peaceful along the riverbanks, the African bush is not a place to let down your guard.

Not far from the Samburu Lodge, we drove down a sandy track to camp near the riverbank. We made certain that the bank was steep enough to prevent any croc from getting any ideas for midnight snacks. As we started to set up our tents, we heard the cracking and ripping of branches coming from somewhere near the river. Cautiously climbing down the steep bank, we were startled to see, directly across the river, fifteen or so elephants gathered around a few acacia trees, the elephants' trunks stretching upward to tear down the branches. Elephants particularly love *Acacia tortilis* seedpods which they eat by the thousands. These seedpods germinate after they pass through the elephants' intestines (acid in the digestive juices eats away at the seed's outer covering) and are

111

then sensitized in the droppings scattered throughout a wide range of territory. Without the elephant's vital role, the *Acacia tortilis* would disappear, perhaps turning the landscape into a wasteland. It is no wonder the elephant is called the "architect of the bush."

We decided to retire early that evening after our dinner. The following day would bring much excitement. We had a lot of territory to cover before reaching the mountain oasis of Marsabit.

# 12

We were already sitting down to breakfast as the sky lightened through the palms near the Uaso Nyiro. We had arisen early to be on the road to reach Marsabit by late afternoon. After breaking camp, we were back on the track through Samburu Reserve, passing the small Samburu Game Lodge that overlooks the river.

When we reached the rangers' post at the Samburu gate, we were on the edge of Samburu tribal country. At first glance, it looked as though we were back in Masai land, since the Samburu are related to the Masai and are the most northerly of all the Maa-speaking tribes. Off in the distance, Samburu boys were leading their large cattle herds and goat flocks, churning up white clouds of dust. Grass huts were perched on high hills overlooking this vast open thornscrub country. At the ranger post hut, we saw a few of the Samburu warriors (*moran*) up close. They are magnificent in appearance, tall and thin, their flame-red togas worn sarong-style on slender frames. Their elaborate hairdos seem to outdo the Masai *moran*. Dyed with ocher, the Samburu hairdos are plaited into visors that shade their eyes, and long braided locks that hang down to their shoulders. Samburu is believed to mean "butterfly," an apt description of these pastoralists who rarely stay in one place for long.

At the rangers' post, the Samburu women had gathered with their trinkets of bracelets, spears, and necklaces, hoping to relieve us of a few shillings. The Samburu may stick to their traditional ways, but they are not averse to drumming up a little twentieth-century retail business from the tourists who stay at the lodge. Much like the Masai women, the Samburu ladies were resplendent in huge, glass-beaded necklaces, metal arm and wrist bracelets, and beaded headbands. Because glass beads, as well as cloth, were the main trade items brought to the East African coast in the twelfth to the nineteenth centuries, the Africans have always coveted glass beads for body adornment. (Back then, the Africans did not know how to make glass.) Today, the Africans get their beads from Europe and, in a twist of irony, they now sell those beads back to the European tourists.

When we checked out at the rangers' post, I noticed a little plaque inside the sentry hut: "In Memory of Elsa Who Helped Safeguard This Game Reserve." Joy and George Adamson donated part of the royalties from *Born Free* to help establish this reserve.

Soon we connected back up with the main Northern Frontier road, heading straight north through the little *duka* town of Archer's Post. From there, Ol Doinyo Sabachi began to grow in front of us as we rumbled over the terrible corrugated road that nearly shook our vehicles to pieces. Here is Africa in the raw, an uncut diamond of true wilderness that had for centuries kept out missionaries, traders, settlers, and other forerunners of civilization until the early 1900s. The first European explorer in the Frontier, the Hungarian Count Samuel Teleki von Szek, led an expedition in the late 1880s of 700 men who faced starvation, hostile nomadic tribes, and unrelenting thirst in this lonely no-man's-land. Close to starvation, Teleki and his men were reduced to climbing trees to rob eggs from bird nests in order to survive. Two hundred of his men never returned from their hellish journey.

Rattling along the corrugation, we often lurched into dips and holes in the road, our heads continually banging against the roof. Every hour or so, we had to stop the vehicles to cool the overheated engines, and to seek the shade of a few acacias, sparsely scattered over the desert. Once when we stopped to change a blown tire on the Land Rover, we were surprised to see one lone bull elephant only a hundred feet off the side of the road. He was slumbering in the shade of a scraggly acacia, his giant ears slowly flapping back and forth, cooling himself off. (When an elephant flaps its ears, blood flows continuously from the body into a network of arteries close to the thin skin surface of the ear, thereby lowering the body temperature by several degrees.)

We marveled at how any living thing could survive in this parched land, let alone a beast the size of an elephant. It is a continual struggle during droughts where all forms of life must learn to adapt—or perish. The desert nomads and their camels must rely on a system of wells (dug 50 feet deep through hard rock) scattered throughout the Frontier. Elephants survive droughts by eating succulent plants, or by digging holes in sandy dry river beds (called *luggas*) to siphon up only a cupful of water at a time. Desert lions can survive weeks without drinking by getting their liquids from their prey. Acacias and bushes survive by storing up water, and the red oat grass has a mechanism in its seeds that twists and turns them into the hard-baked earth.

Surprisingly, in this desolate land there are road hazards, first appearing as tornadoes of dust, gradually building up on the road to take the shape of a huge truck barreling along at top speed, the horn blasting, forcing you off the road. The trucks were invariably loaded with hundreds of bouncing crates of empty Coca-Cola bottles that rattled deafeningly by us. The madcap African drivers keep the little Frontier *duka* towns continually replenished with Coca-Cola from a Nairobi bottling company. We wondered how even one bottle could ever survive such a punishment.

Other road hazards were less intimidating. Out of nowhere, a purple-legged Somali ostrich came tearing into the middle of the road, stopped, did a double-take at our vehicles, and then took off again. Instead of running to the side of the road to get out of the way, the big bird with the itty-bitty brain decided to trot along smack in the middle of the road, its long legs kicking up puffs of dust. The faster we'd go, the faster the ostrich would accelerate. The ostrich pranced ahead of us like a band majorette for a couple of miles. When we stopped the vehicles, it finally made a quick right turn back into the bush.

As we vibrated along the road, we could only think of cooling drinks and shaded forest once we reached Marsabit. We were worn to a frazzle in the 100 degree-plus temperatures. But several hours or so after having left Archer's Post at Samburu Reserve, our eyes rested on a green mound of hills on the horizon to the north. As we drove closer, the hills began to rise dramatically in height like a giant coiled green serpent. It was the foothills of Mount Marsabit.

A forested mountain in the middle of a desert is a strange phenomenon. Marsabit's forest vegetation is created by the monsoon winds that blow inland from the coast and then meet up with the 5,990-foot volcanic mountain obstruction. Consequently, the slopes receive sufficient rainfall to create a lush growth. It is no wonder that Marsabit has been like a magnet to generations of nomads and their camel caravans, who sought the dark cool forests and mountain walls above the blazing sands and scorching lava rocks.

A couple of hours later, we began to leave the Kaisut Desert behind as we drove up into the gentler grassy slopes of Marsabit. The road coiled around the mountain, splitting two starkly different worlds in half: to our left, the Chalbi Desert radiated in the merciless sun far in the distance; to our right, a wall of olive-green forest (covering 60 square miles) was draped with silvery moss that blew in the wind like witches' tresses.

On the road we passed many people of the Rendille tribe with their camels, as well as Samburu people with their goats and sheep. Soon the winding road led us into the little shanty

Samburu shepherd boys of Northern Frontier deserts watch over their large flocks of goats.

Colorful Samburu women gather to sell beads, necklaces, and bracelets at the ranger's post of Samburu Reserve.

Desert nomads of Kenya's Northern Frontier lead their camel caravans up the slopes of the foothills of Mount Marsabit.

*Left:* At the Singing Wells of Marsabit, nomad women load up their pack donkeys for the journey back up the gorge.

*Right:* The rhythmic ➤ chanting of "Oola, oola, oola" reverberates off the walls as men and women pass buckets from the wells to the watering troughs.

The track leads up through the misty forest of Marsabit toward Lake Paradise.

Lake Paradise and the ancient elephant trail. The Kaisut Desert shimmers in the distance.

Martin Johnson looked a bit shaken after Osa shot elephant that charged the camera while he was filming it. Reruns of the old Johnson movies inspired me to operate bush safaris.

Pert little Osa Johnson pauses before their Lake Paradise home on a rainy day and smiles back at her husband.

Camping among the buttressed trees at Marsabit near Lake Paradise.

Duba, the Borana boy, tears away vegetation revealing the foundation stones of Martin and Osa Johnson's house at Lake Paradise. Marsabit forest has long since reclaimed site where their compound was built.

Lions in Northern Kenya, a rainbow behind them.

The sky appears to have caught on fire over Lake Turkana.

town of Marsabit, lined with corrugated tin shacks and *dukas*. At the end of town, we found a little hostel at the very edge of the Marsabit forest and decided to camp there for the night so as to explore the little town. The next morning we'd enter Marsabit Reserve.

We set up our tents in a little wooded area that enclosed the campsite and the cement building of the hostel. The camp is a mile below the edge of the dense forest which rises sharply up a steep slope. As soon as we unloaded the vehicles, two teen-age African boys of the Borana tribe raced up to us to collect their shillings for camping fees. The Borana boys, named Duba and Abdul, decided to be the self-appointed guides to Marsabit forest. Elaine, the ever-doting grandmother, immediately "adopted" the Borana boys, who began to set up her tent. They complimented Elaine on her bright orange hair, but they stared hard at her, puzzled as to why this grandmother did not have gray hair.

"Don't you dare breathe a word about my dyeing my hair," Elaine warned us under her breath. "If the boys find out there are gray roots, they might leave me out for the hyenas."

After dark when the camp was set up, the boys invited us into their little restaurant inside the hostel. Since their fathers had been away for a few days—but would return the following day—the boys had had the responsibility of all the work of running the little business. At a table lit by kerosene lanterns, we were served roast goat meat, buttered bread and jam, and pots of sugary, milky tea. Eating goat meat is like chewing an old boot, but we smiled at the boys, telling them it was delicious as we chewed and chewed and chewed. The boys beamed toothy smiles, believing we were merely savoring our supper.

Abdul and Duba said that we could have baths because there was a large six-foot-high water tank with a spigot right behind the hostel. The boys furnished a large tin basin with which a person could have a sponge bath.

Jack, Brian, Pete, Aya, Ulla, and I decided to stroll into the town to have a look around. Abdul and Duba, of course, appointed themselves the town guides. Elaine, though, decided to stay behind to have a sponge bath at the water tank after everyone had left. The boys warned her that the spigot on the tank sometimes sticks.

We strolled down the one-street town, the little *dukas* lit by scores of kerosene lanterns. We entered one dark *duka* to have warm beers. The African woman who owned the shop had a prehistoric record player and only one scratchy record. She played Glenn Miller's "In the Mood" over and over again. Not in the mood for one more playing of that, we decided to head back to the hostel.

Since the moon was not yet up, we groped our way up the pitch-black pathway, following our flashlight beams back to the campsite. Arriving at the hostel, we became anxious. There was no sign or sound of Elaine. No lights had been turned on in the vehicles under the trees. We got a little spooked.

Just then we heard muffled crying that seemed to come from behind the water tank. "Elaine, is that you?" I called out into the blackness.

"Thank God, you're back!" came a quavery voice from behind the tank. When we walked to the other side of the water tank, we shone our flashlights and Elaine emerged into the light—or what remotely looked like Elaine. She was covered from head to toe in thick, black mud, her flowered muumuu hung on her like a soaked rag, her face and hair were black as crude oil, and only the whites of her eyes showed through. Elaine looked like the tar baby from *The Adventures of Brer Rabbit*.

"Oh, Mama!" an alarmed Abdul and Duba cried out. "What happened to you?"

"It was awful," Elaine said, big tears streaming down her muddied face. "Soon after you left, I took off all my clothes in the dark and started to take my sponge bath. After I turned on the spigot and lathered my body with soap, my flashlight died . . . just as I heard African men talking, coming up the dark path following beams from flashlights. I couldn't find my muu-muu in the dark, so I trotted behind the water tank stark naked and held my breath, not making a sound. After the men passed by, I tried to rinse off the soap but the spigot got stuck. Then I heard more men's voices coming up the path, and again I trotted behind the tank. I started to cry silently, since I couldn't see a thing, and I was starting to shiver from the soapy water. After those men passed by, I felt around for the water pan, stood up, and lifted it over my head and poured the rinse water over me. But the shock of ice cold water made me lose my balance and I slipped and fell face-first into the slop of mud. I quickly put on my soaked muu-muu when I heard you call out. I'm a mess!"

Abdul and Duba immediately went into the hostel, lit lamps, and started to boil water for tea. "Poor Mama, Poor Mama," the boys kept saying, shaking their heads. As we sipped our tea in the lantern light, Orange Blossom tried to towel off some of the mud.

Much later, Elaine made a wonderful joke out of the whole thing, wondering what would have happened had those African men been surprised by a naked white lady, with orange hair, suddenly emerging from a mud wallow.

"They'd probably be halfway across the Chalbi Desert by now," Jack said. It was the first time I saw tears of laughter well up in Jack's eyes. Elaine was passing Kleenex around to everybody.

Just before first light, a riot of roosters throughout Marsabit town cranked up, forcing us to crawl out of our warm cocoons in the chilling air. Abdul and Duba already had pots of steaming tea boiling away on several *jiko* charcoal stoves. Shivering in the nippy air, we all stumbled out of our tents and headed into the hostel. The boys served us eggs and bread, and said they wanted to take us to the Singing Wells just outside of town.

"*Singing* wells?" Elaine looked puzzled.

Abdul and Duba said it would be a surprise, something that is seldom seen by outsiders.

After breakfast we climbed into our vehicles and the boys guided us to the edge of the village, past the open market, and down a narrow track. Five miles out of town, we looked back and could see the edge of the forest above the *dukas*. The road wound through large fields of maize and small *shambas*. "Let's stop here for a second," Duba said. "I want to show you something."

When we got out of the vehicles, we walked through stalks of maize, and then suddenly the fields ended at the brink of a seven-foot-deep trench that stretched like a dry riverbed through the field. I thought the town must be putting in a new water drainage ditch.

"That's for the elephants," Duba said. "At night, elephants come out of the forest to raid the maize and sweet potato crops. Because Marsabit town is growing, the government dug this fifteen-foot-wide trench that runs for several miles, to keep out the elephants. But elephants are too smart, and in some places they merely push dirt into the trench and walk over it."

"I wonder," Elaine smiled, "whether some offspring of the elephant Martin and Osa Johnson called Sweet Potato, the one who nightly raided Osa's garden, has picked up Sweet Potato's habit of midnight raids."

Back inside the vehicles, we continued down the narrow track. After a mile or so, the trees disappeared and we found ourselves at the edge of a 400-foot-deep rocky gorge. Clouds of dust obliterated the gorge bottom where hundreds of cattle, sheep, and goats were working their way up and down the steep cliff sides in single file. Men and women of the Borana tribe were leading their pack donkeys up and down the age-old trails worn through rock. The donkeys brayed loudly, complaining of their heavy burdens of leather water containers and plastic jerry cans strapped to their backs.

When we parked the vehicles at the cliff's edge, we could faintly hear the chanting of the Africans below, their voices carried up on the wind. "*Oola, Oola, Oola, Oola,*" The Africans beat out the rhythmic chanting that echoed off the gorge walls continuously, as though the songs through the centuries had never once ceased. We had arrived at the Singing Wells—appropriately called the Oolanoola wells by the Africans.

After picking our way over the rocks down to the bottom of the steep gorge, we were in the midst of a storm of noise and activity. Scores of people of the Borana tribe were shouting at their cattle, which were climbing over the backs of sheep and goats, trying to find a drinking place among the water troughs molded from hardened mud.

When we walked over to one of the wells, we peered down to see a human pillar of men and women, standing one above the other on rock steps cut into the walls of the well. "*Oola! Oola!*" The chants beat like a pulsating heart, as the Africans stood on their ladder of rock ledges, passing giraffe-hide buckets from hand to hand up the human tower like firemen on a water brigade. Their arms moved in precision with the chants, working like the legs of a centipede as buckets were passed up and down the well, while the man at the top poured water into the troughs. He could barely keep pace with the cattle, sheep, and goats that sucked up the water like vacuums. The "*Oola! Oola!*" chants would suddenly quicken in pace to a staccato rhythm, the buckets now a blur of motion, flying up and down the well on hands working away like an assembly line on fast-forward.

For centuries the Rendille and Samburu tribes (and of more recent times, the Borana) have brought their cattle, sheep, goats, or camels to the system of wells at the lower slopes of Marsabit mountain. This age-old scene stays with you long after the nomads have moved back up the gorge with their pack donkeys.

As we looked straight up the steep walls to the south of

the gorge, we noticed the startling contrast towering above us: the edge of the silver-green forest wall. We would enter the forest road to Lake Paradise to set up camp by late afternoon. But first, Duba and Abdul wanted to take us to a Borana village several miles north of Marsabit town.

We drove back on the same narrow track past maize fields and then on to a green velvet carpet of open grass country of the Borana compounds. Many beehive-shaped grass huts were scattered about on the foothills north of the mountain. As soon as we entered one of the Borana temporary settlements, we stopped the vehicles near a cluster of huts. An older Borana man and several women greeted Abdul and Duba. The Borana elder was dressed in a white *kikoi*, with a white cloak wrapped around his shoulders. The women were stunning, wearing long colorful dresses, aluminum beads and jewelry, their hair done up in tight corn braids that set off their fine features and brown skin. The older man, who was the head man of the settlement (considered a titular father; the Borana have no chiefs), welcomed us to share a meal with him and his family. But before going into his hut, the headman wanted to show us around. Considerable numbers of cattle and camels were grazing and browsing on the hills that rolled down to the desert, which stretched onto and through the Ethiopian border some eighty miles to the north.

Generations ago, the Borana (the largest Galla-speaking tribe in Kenya) migrated down from the Ethiopian highlands to adopt a pastoral way of life in northern Kenya. Although traditionally cattle herders, the Borana now are becoming more of a camel economy, since they lost most of their cattle during the Somali *shifta* (bandit) raids of the 1960s.

Walking through the settlement, we observed several women milking the camels. The Borana subsist mainly on the camels' milk, as well as goat meat and maize to supplement their diet. However, like most nomadic tribes, the threat of droughts forever hangs over their heads; they may lose most of their livestock within only a few months. This is why some

Borana have shunned their traditional ways of life and have sought to find work in Marsabit town.

When we returned to the huts, the Borana headman told Abdul and Duba that his wife was not feeling well, and wondered whether we might have some medicine with us. Aya and Ulla said they would take a look at his wife.

After we followed the headman into his dark hut, it took some time for our eyes to adjust. His wife was sitting on a small wooden stool holding a tiny baby. Aya and Ulla then checked the woman over and decided she had a slightly upset stomach.

"Wait a minute," Elaine said. "I think I have a solution to the problem in my duffel bag. An *African* solution, if you will. Just watch for awhile."

While Elaine went back to the Land Rover, we had an opportunity to observe the hut. The inside was surprisingly cool, but full of choking smoke which keeps out the insects. A small charcoal fire was boiling up a large pan of milky tea. The hut was cluttered with wooden stools, wooden bowls, giraffe-hide buckets, and wooden beds covered with animal hides. Woven grass mats had been placed over the dirt floor.

The headman motioned for us to sit on the little wooden stools, since he wanted us to stay to eat. Duba said some of the women had prepared something special for us. When we asked what that something special was, he smiled at us innocently, and said, "Goat meat!" We all gulped and forced toothy smiles.

"I found the medicine," Elaine said, reentering the hut. "Can you get me a gourd of water, please?"

When Duba handed Elaine the gourd, she sat down on a stool in front of the elder's wife. She waved one hand back and forth over the water vessel on the floor. Then, almost imperceptively, I saw Elaine open her right fist and secretly sprinkle white powder into the gourd. The water immediately began to fizz and bubble.

The Borana headman and his wife watched wide-eyed as

Elaine did her hocus-pocus over the water. She motioned for the woman to drink it straight down in one gulp. Then, the woman burped—one hefty burp you could hear all over.

Even Jack could barely contain himself from laughing. "Oh, brother," he rolled his eyes at Elaine. "Who died and left you Witch Doctor?"

"Just an American remedy . . . Bromo Seltzer," Elaine smiled. "And a little African voodoo. We'll wait to see what happens."

The Borana headman now ordered two small boys to bring the roasted goat meat and camel's milk. When they returned with the food, and we tried the camel's milk, we were surprised to find it tasty and sweet. Our teeth flashed as we chewed and ground the goat meat, and it made us look as if we were smiling, wanting more—making the headman pile more into our bowls. As is true with Africans, hospitality is a most valued custom for guests. The more we chewed and chewed, showing our teeth, the more goat meat he heaped into our bowls.

When we finally, and gratefully, finished the goat meat, Abdul and Duba said we should get moving to set up camp at Lake Paradise by late afternoon. When we thanked the headman and his wife, Duba told us that the headman's wife no longer had her stomachache. Of course, Elaine was pleased. "Just call me *Daktari* Elaine," she laughed.

As we drove off past the settlements and maize fields, our eyes were drawn toward the distant mountain of Marsabit. Lake Paradise awaited us.

# 13

IN MARSABIT TOWN, we stopped at the open-air village market to buy fresh vegetables and several freshly cut-up chickens. Then, we returned to the hostel to load up our gear. Abdul and Duba continued to be our guides.

It was only a mile or so ride up a track to the edge of the forest. Since Marsabit had not yet been declared a national park, there was no rangers' post at the forest edge. Better yet, there were no tourists. We'd have Lake Paradise all to ourselves.

Only an old, rotting wood marker pointed the way to the crater lake.

As we drove up the narrow tree-lined track, the forest became denser the higher our vehicles climbed. Even though the seasonal short rains had ended, occasional showers had kept the track greasy with mud. Vehicles that had struggled through the mud a few days before had left deep ruts in the track, making the going even tougher. Although we saw no game, we did see elephant droppings on the track. The olive, croton, and cordia trees became denser, covered with vines that crept up the 100-foot-high trunks. Shafts of sunlight filtered through the green cathedral. Strong whiffs of humus and vegetation were a welcome change from the choking dust of the deserts that surround Marsabit.

"I know this might sound corny," Elaine said, "but my

adrenaline is pumping in anticipation of getting my first glimpse of Lake Paradise."

Fifteen minutes later, our vehicles struggled higher and higher up a track at a near 45-degree angle, and the forest became even more lush. The first white man to see this was an American explorer, Arthur Donaldson Smith who, in 1895, had trekked eastward across the Chalbi Desert from Lake Rudolf (now Lake Turkana) with seventy porters. Two years later, in 1897, Lord Delamere also explored and mar-veled at this mountain oasis in a desert. He was also impressed with Marsabit's large elephants that carried monstrous-sized tusks.

Jack shifted the Land Rover into four-wheel drive, the gears grinding and groaning until we climbed the track to a flat level. Looking behind us, there was no sign of the van. We climbed out of the Rover and walked back down the forest track and saw the van stopped halfway down.

"Well, here comes the pushing part," Jack grumbled. "It looks as though we'll have to work hard to pay our dues to get into Paradise."

Brian, Abdul, and Duba were pushing the van from the rear as Pete drove, straining the first gear, coaxing the van up the incline over the ruts.

"Okay, everybody," Jack rallied us all behind the van. "Let's employ the Kenyan laborers' rallying cry for 'let us all pull together.' *Harambee!*"

"Haram-BAY! Haram-BAY!" we all grunted as we strained against the van to get some rhythm and sweat worked up. Gradually, like Egyptian slaves moving a giant stone of a pyramid, we inched the van up the hill to a flat level.

After we caught our breath, we climbed back in the vehicles only to confront more steep hills, then down inclines, then up again through the dense forest. About an hour later, we groaned in frustration as we confronted yet another steep incline.

Since we were a few thousand feet in elevation above the

desert floor, the forest vegetation changed dramatically. The undergrowth had thinned out, and the trees had become thicker with gnarled trunks, their branches festooned with Spanish moss. Looking straight up the track, we could see an opening of clear blue sky at the top of the hill.

Since the van was beginning to wheeze and lag behind, Jack connected it to a steel cable. We added a little more "*Harambee*" behind the van, as the Rover's engine screamed with the extra weight. Inch by inch by inch, the wheels spinning madly, tossing mud, we laboriously pushed the van the extra inch to the top of the incline. We at once found ourselves in a grassy clearing of bright sunshine where a few gnarled trees were scattered about.

But nothing had prepared us for the sudden ripping aside of the trees to our left that exposed the gaping mouth of Gof Sokorte Guda crater lake, 300 feet straight down from the edge of the cliff. At last, after all those years of holding onto a dream, I had arrived at Lake Paradise!

We stepped out of the vehicles and walked to the cliff edge. We gazed down in wonderment at the one-square-mile, spoon-shaped Lake Paradise, surrounded by a grassy shoreline that sloped up to thick forest. A mile and a half in the distance, a wide elephant trail cut through the forest, leading out onto the grassy shoreline to the lake's edge.

The contrast between forest mountain and desert was startling. Seen over and beyond the highest ridge of trees lining the crater's rim across from us, the reddish-brown expanse of the Kaisut Desert stretched from the mountain's base toward a distant horizon lost in haze. A strong wind was moaning through the hoary twisted trunks of the buttressed trees that clacked throughout the forest surrounding the lake. For some, the wind seemed to carry a faint voice from the past: "It's a paradise, Martin!"

Noticing a cluster of black dots near the shore, I picked up my binoculars and focused on some seventy buffaloes grazing near the water. The lake edge was choked with blue and white water lilies. Hundreds of white butterflies flitted across the water like confetti tossed to the wind. The calls of ducks, geese, and egrets were carried on the wind that blew tresses of Spanish moss that was draped all over the buttressed trees on the crater rim.

"I don't know about you, Richard," Elaine said, "but I have goosebumps. It looks exactly as I imagined it."

I went to the Land Rover and got out my old copy of Osa Johnson's *Four Years in Paradise* to compare Martin's photo of the lake taken in the 1920s. The picture revealed that it had been taken from the same spot where we now stood. The old photograph showed the tops of thatched houses on a rise to our right, just above the elephant trail. Through the years since then, the forest has reclaimed the Johnsons' compound and movie film laboratory.

"Tomorrow morning," Elaine said excitedly, "let's explore the Johnsons' old site and see whether we might find some remains of their house and other buildings. Who knows what we might discover?"

It was about 4:30 P.M. when we decided to move on, to follow the narrow elephant track down through the forest and out onto the grassy shoreline at the lake's edge. There, beside Lake Paradise, surrounded by the forested walls of the crater lake, we would set up camp. As we started to head back to the vehicles, Jack thought he saw something through his binoculars. We all picked up our own binoculars and noticed a large figure, like a huge gray rock, moving down the old elephant trail. The "rock" suddenly took form as a lone elephant emerging from the trail heading toward the lake. Within minutes, more elephants began to blacken the trail, keeping their age-old appointment for a late afternoon drink and a bath. Within another half hour, the lakeshore was crowded with more than 80 elephants. Some of the herd began to wade knee-deep in the lake.

Elaine was silent as she watched the elephants through her binoculars. I could see she was deeply moved as she turned to me. "How truly lucky we are," she said. "Just think of the people in the world who will never see this."

It was remarkable, that after all these years, Lake Paradise had remained virtually unchanged since the Johnsons had lived here. We could imagine the Johnsons' enormous expedition of safari cars, as hundreds of Africans ahead of them, hacked the trail through the forest to the lake. In the 1920s it was one of the largest safaris ever organized, with five mule-drawn wagons, four ox carts, four trucks, six overloaded Willys-Knight cars, and 230 African porters who carried 255 crates of supplies and $50,000 worth of camera equipment.

Before we realized it, we had been "elephant watching" for nearly an hour. Jack urged us to get moving before dark to set up camp. We got back in the vehicles, and followed the track along the crater rim. We passed the site of the Johnson compound, that was now nothing but trees and underbrush. There was no sign that anyone ever lived here.

The track connected up with the wide elephant trail that led us down to the lake's shoreline. Thankfully for the moment, the elephants were two hundred yards away, across the lake.

Within the hour, we had the camp set up, placing the tents so that they faced the elephant trail. There was a delicious feeling of apprehension, wondering if we would be surprised by elephants walking past our tents in the dark. Aya did not quite share our excitement about elephants.

The rays of the setting sun now tinged the tops of the trees above us with golden light. Within minutes, the forest turned black, and the temperatures seemed to drop as fast as the sun. We shone our flashlights onto the lake, and the herd was beginning slowly to move off in another direction into the forest.

By the light of a kerosene lamp on her kitchen worktable, Elaine had her nose buried in Osa Johnson's book, checking out Osa's recipe for wild buffalo oxtail soup. We asked her how in the world she could duplicate a wild buffalo soup.

"You cheat a lot," she answered. "Knorr's packaged oxtail soup will do. I've found Osa's recipe for sauce for fried chicken and her sweet potatoes."

After Aya and Ulla had set the table, Jack and I lit the lanterns and candles, while the others helped Elaine. Duba and Abdul filled the pitchers with fresh water.

About ninety minutes later we gathered around the table to sit down to our "Johnson dinner" at Lake Paradise. Just a couple of hundred feet above us on the cliff top, the Johnsons' house once stood overlooking the lake. Surrounding us, Marsabit forest was hauntingly hushed, and it was easy to turn back the pages of time to imagine a light burning late in Martin's laboratory as he developed movie film he had shot only hours earlier. After a long day in the lab, Martin often took the short walk back to his Paradise house to find a fire blazing in the hearth. Wearing an elegant pair of satin pajamas, and with her hair bobbed, pretty Osa would light candles on a linen-spread table and pour vintage wine into crystal goblets. Dinner might consist of caviar, freshly baked bread, candied sweet potatoes, wild buffalo oxtail soup, and roast guinea fowl, followed by homemade strawberry ice cream. After Martin and Osa retired for the evening, a certain six-ton elephant would usually be right on schedule to sneak into the compound, and make his way past the watermelons to the sweet potato patch. After dining there with his eyes closed, Sweet Potato, as the Johnsons referred to the beast, would dissolve back into the forest as silently as he had arrived.

Our own Paradise night was magic at our candlelit table. Elaine had prepared Osa's menu to perfection: oxtail soup with garden vegetables; fried chicken with a cream sauce flavored with pepper, parsley, onion juice, and fresh mushrooms; candied sweet potatoes; celery hearts; garden-fresh salad; and onions au gratin.

"Don't start eating yet! You've got to wait for my surprise!" Elaine said as she went over to the Land Rover to dig in her duffel bag.

A minute later she returned to the table with a large bottle.

"French champagne!" Aya and Ulla exclaimed, staring in disbelief.

"I swear Orange Blossom has *everything* in that duffel bag!" Jack said, trying to hide his pleasure.

"But, of course," Elaine said. "Osa sometimes served champagne on special occasions. We will have a toast to the Johnsons and to the magnificence of this unchanged paradise."

Brian and Pete remembered we had a few Coca-Colas to give Abdul and Duba so that they could share in the toast. Although the boys had been in the forest many times before, they had never had the opportunity to camp on a safari overnight at Paradise. They were all eyes, fascinated by all the equipment we carried with us on safari.

A loud pop from the cork echoed into the night. Champagne frothed over from the bottle as Jack poured "the bubbly" into our glasses. We raised them to the memory of the Johnsons.

Since our safari would come to an end a few days after camping at Lake Turkana and then heading straight back to Nairobi, Elaine proposed a toast to all of us: "I hate to see this safari come to an end. I wish we could go on forever. It has been grand sharing all of this with you. You know, if I climbed a hill to see the most wonderful African sunset, but couldn't share it with someone, I think I would turn my back on it and walk back down the hill."

Just before eating, we put on sweaters as the temperature dropped at this 4,500-foot elevation. The chilly night air gave us more of an appetite. Elaine heaped the food on Abdul's and Duba's plates to overflowing. "I never want to see kids hungry," she said. "There's plenty for second and third helpings." Abdul's and Duba's stomachs were bottomless pits.

After dinner, we had to put on parkas over our sweaters

as the temperature continued to drop. We blew out the candles and turned down the kerosene lanterns. At once, we were bathed in a shower of glittering stars, looking as though they'd been ensnared on the branches of the forest trees. The wind started up. The creaking and clacking of the gnarled buttressed trees and the soft swishing of leaves were the only sounds in the crater.

After we had cleared the table, washed the dishes, and put everything away, we decided to stargaze for awhile and wait for a nearly full moon to drift over the forest. Bundling up in more sweaters, we sat in our chairs in front of our tents. Every so often we switched our flashlights onto the elephant trail—just in case.

As though some mythical giant were carrying a lantern through the forest, the sky lightened faintly above the outline of trees along the crater rim, directly across the lake from us. Slowly, the edge of the moon peaked above the tree line, and rose above the forest, blotting out some of the stars. The face on the moon stared at its own reflection in the lake.

After everyone else had retired inside their tents for the night, I decided to have one last cup of tea and then crawl into my sleeping bag, placed outside the tent. It was in the wee hours of the night, when I woke up suddenly with the feeling something was watching me. In the shadows of the silver light, I saw a doglike figure standing six feet from me. I quickly switched on my torch and then let out a yell. The flashlight picked up the reflection of two eyes. A striped hyena spun around and bolted across the elephant trail in the moonlight, his shaggy coat and tail flying in the wind as he slunk back into the forest. My startled companions awakened, wondering if I had seen elephants. I told them it was a snooping hyena. I was not at ease, knowing that hyenas eat anything, including leather boots. I was hoping that this hyena had not been planning on eating my shoes—with my feet attached. I moved back into my tent.

———

When I awoke in the early morning light, the birds were already chattering in the trees above the camp. I opened the tent flap and was surprised to see a heavy mantle of mist covering the crater, completely obliterating the lake.

"Hey! Where did the lake go to?" the others asked as they stood in front of their tents yawning and stretching. "It looks like we're standing in the middle of a cloud."

Later when we sat down to breakfast, shivering in the cold, we watched the mist lighten as the sun cut through. Elaine was in a hurry to eat since she was excited about exploring the site of the Johnsons' old compound. "We have some archeological work to do, Richard," she said. "Let's get a move on."

Duba decided to accompany Elaine and me as the others cleaned up and began to load the vehicles. "Don't forget Osa's *Paradise* book," Elaine said as we started up the hill on the elephant trail. We walked up a few hundred feet, and reached the open grassy area where buttressed trees overlooked the lake.

We were a little apprehensive as we walked through the waist-high grass, hoping that we wouldn't disturb any snakes. When we walked to the cliff's edge, we opened Osa's book to look at the pictures of the Johnsons' compound. We thought we might be standing near the exact spot where the Johnsons' house stood. But we could see nothing in the high grass. Duba was walking a hundred feet off through the grass where Osa's garden was once located. He then combed the area where Martin's laboratory was situated.

"I really don't think we're going to find anything," I said to a disappointed Elaine, who was determined to keep on looking. For an hour we scoured the grass, but I believed too many years had gone by and nature had completely reclaimed the site. We were just about to give up when we heard Duba yell. "Over here! I think I've found something!"

We ran over to Duba, who was pulling up grass from a mound of dirt. As we helped Duba clear more grass and dirt away, we noticed several rocks. Digging with our fingers into the dirt, we realized the "rocks" were actually roughly made gray blocks, layered one on top of the other. With joy, we realized we were uncovering foundation stones of one of the old buildings. Elaine believed there must still be some remains of their home, and we returned to the edge of the cliff. We walked down a little hill and thought we saw what looked like a wall. Pulling the dirt and grass away, we exposed a brick wall that was five feet or so high. Since this wall was at the cliff's edge, we knew we were looking at the foundations of the Johnsons' old house and stone veranda that overlooked the lake.

"If you remember the *Paradise* book, you'll recall that Osa made these bricks with her own hands," Elaine said, her eyes big with wonder. "And, here, this wall has remained after all this time since the 1920s."

When we walked farther down the hill, we laughed when we saw scores of loose, crumbling bricks, tumbled about the hillside in plain sight, just for the picking. These bricks were most likely the remains of the large fireplace the Johnsons had inside their home. For Elaine and me, these bricks could just have well been buried treasure. And, of course, Elaine insisted on having one as a souvenir. Duba scraped two bricks away from the top of the wall, and gave them to us. We felt like a couple of kids.

In the distance we could hear the engines of the vehicles coming up the elephant track. We walked triumphantly onto the road, holding our bricks as if they were gold bars from Fort Knox.

When the Land Rover pulled up, Jack smiled at Elaine. "So, Orange Blossom, you have found your dream."

Our companions stepped out of the vehicles and had to have a look at the foundation walls of the compound. In my imagination, I could plainly see Osa in her garden, wearing her wide-brimmed safari hat, planting vegetables from seeds she'd brought from Kansas. The Johnsons had lived the idyllic life on Marsabit mountain.

That life was tragically cut short only ten years after the couple left Marsabit in 1927. The Johnsons were in a commercial plane crash in California in 1937. Although Martin died a few days later in the hospital, Osa miraculously survived her injuries from the crash, after a long recuperation. In the years left to her, she turned out books about their adventures, and went on the lecture circuit. In 1953, Osa suffered a heart attack and died alone in her New York apartment. Up to the day of her death, Osa mourned Martin, and was haunted by the memories of her Lake Paradise home so very far away. Fortunately for posterity, the old Johnson movies and other safari memorabilia—the ultimate documentation of wilderness areas that no longer exist—are preserved at the Martin and Osa Johnson Safari Museum in Chanute, Kansas, Osa's hometown.

As we climbed back into the vehicles, we left the old Johnson site, and followed the track along the edge of the crater rim. We decided to stop and have one last look down at the lake. We sat for an hour on the cliff top, silently contemplating Paradise.

In 1927, when the time had come for the Johnsons to leave Marsabit, Osa had looked out over the lovely lake, and the ancient elephant trail, and said a little prayer, asking the Almighty to protect the place forever as a sanctuary for wildlife. Then they made the long descent from their beloved mountain home for the last time.

As we began to drive back down the mountain track, I was grateful that Marsabit had remained a Paradise. For now, it appeared, Osa's prayer had been answered after all.

CHAPTER

# 14

AFTER LEAVING MARSABIT FOREST, we dropped Abdul and Duba off at the hostel and paid them for their guide services. The boys hated to see us leave. They gave Elaine a big hug as she rummaged through her bag looking for Kleenex. "Don't feel sad, Mama," they consoled her. "We know some day you'll come back."

Within the hour we were braking the vehicles down a steep rocky road that overlooked the vast white expanse of the salt flats of the Chalbi Desert. When we reached the desert, the temperature began to soar upward toward 120 degrees as the sun blinded us in its intensity. The green rolling slopes of Mount Marsabit behind us gradually flattened out on the horizon as we rumbled over rocks and sand, farther into the Chalbi.

An hour or so later our vehicles reached the thin crust of the salt flats, the tires slowly sinking deeper into the sands. Although the crust looks rock solid, it is deceptive. Surprisingly, the Chalbi Desert does have flash rain storms that turn the sand into ponds of muddy slop. When the crust dries in the sun, the sand beneath remains wet. During flash floods, dry riverbeds to the south can suddenly turn into torrential rivers, with a six-foot wall of water sweeping everything out of its path—even large trucks that have gotten stuck in the sand.

136

Before long, our vehicles became stuck in sand and salt up to their axles. We climbed out into the 120-degree heat that blew across the desert like a blast furnace, and started to shovel the sand out from under the tires, often digging with our hands under the axles.

Once again, we employed our *"Harambee!"* pushing-and-groaning rhythms as we slowly budged the vehicles onto harder ground. We would travel on for a few more miles, and then hopelessly find ourselves digging again. Elaine kept filling our cups as we gulped down quarts of water at a time.

Jack and I now used the sand tracks (long metal sheets with studded steel grips) to slip under the tires. Eventually, we had to use the Land Rover steel cables to haul the van over the soft sand until we reached rocky, hard ground. Once out of the salt flats, we picked up speed and roared fast over the Chalbi to circulate air through the vehicles.

The farther we drove into the desert, the more we would come across long camel caravans of the Rendille tribe. The long lines of camels looked like fleets of sailing ships on a bleached ocean. The Rendille do not ride on their camels, but load all their household possessions on the camels' backs. The long, curved poles—which are the framework for the Rendille huts covered with camel hides—stick up high on the camels' backs like the masts of ships.

By late afternoon, we came upon an oasis of palm trees and shrubs in the middle of the sand. The sun was now rapidly dropping behind the distant hills. We were never so glad to see the sun set in our lives. The temperatures immediately dropped as the wind suddenly stopped blowing across the iron-flat desert. We were so exhausted that we could only drink endless cups of tea and nibble on cheese and bread. No wonder the nomads rely on tea as a tonic to get them through the desert.

Since there were mercifully no mosquitoes, we decided to just roll our sleeping bags out on the sands. A shatter of stars sprinkled down from the heavens to the horizon that circled us. We felt like we were on the floor of an enormous glittering dome.

"I've never experienced complete, *total* silence before!" Elaine marveled. "No wind—nothing. It's like a void. An eerie silence—like being at the end of the earth."

A few hours after we fell asleep, we awakened to see a full moon above the desert. The sand glowed, seeming to turn night into day.

Before the crack of dawn we were back on the road to cover more miles before the sun came up. After traveling some five hours across coal-black lava beds scattered about the landscape like giant bowling balls, the heat intensified. The ground temperature on the blistered lava rocks and cinder cones can reach 150 degrees by mid-afternoon. Mirages of lakes and mountains shimmered on the horizon. Although no vegetation is seen, we were surprised to see a few lonely camels crossing the lava beds, evidently having wandered away from some nomads' encampments. A camel can survive ten days or longer without drinking, getting some liquid from sparse vegetation. Once a camel drinks, it can consume 50 gallons of water in one day.

Our vehicles climbed to the top of one lava bed, and we were surprised to suddenly come upon a stretch of turquoise water ten miles in the distance far below. It wasn't a mirage this time, but a section of the vast expanse of the 180-mile-long Lake Turkana, the largest alkaline lake in the world. Sodium carbonate in the brackish water is conducive to growing algae, which in turn gives the lake a bluish-green color. Hence, Turkana is appropriately called the Jade Sea. It is believed that this lake once escaped into the Nile River, but centuries ago it became cut off from the Nile and now has no outlet. It is fed by the Omo River to the north.

As we bumped along over the lava rocks, the vehicles' engines continued to overheat, forcing us to stop. We had a choice: either stay inside the vehicles and bake, or step outside and be blowtorched by the sledgehammer sun. It was the classic case of frying pan or the fire.

The first European to trek this inferno was Count Teleki in 1888. He found the great desert lake and named it Lake Rudolf after one of the patrons of the expedition, Prince Rudolf, the crown prince of Austria. Teleki wrote of numbers of elephants that lived around the desert lake. It is hard to imagine an elephant surviving among the lava beds. It attests to the great beast's adaptive process.

The cool waters of Turkana were now tantalizingly close. After slowly lurching over the lava rocks down the steep track, we arrived a couple of hours later at the shores of the Jade Sea. The water beckoned our mummified bodies. Spotting a flattened area near the shore for camping, we immediately walked onto the hot rocks and spike grass to plunge into the lake. Since the lake evaporates in the heat two inches per day, the evaporation cools the brackish soda water down to a cool bath. Although there are many crocodiles in Lake Turkana, they are found more to the north, since they have been hunted by the Ol Molo fishermen. We were in heaven as we splashed about in the water.

We decided this would be the perfect setting to have our safari "Farewell Evening" before heading south from the lake tomorrow for the three-day trip back to Nairobi.

After we set up camp, we drove into the little oasis village of Loyangalani near the foot of Mount Kulal. There we bought a twenty-pound Nile perch from one of the Ol Molo fishermen, a tribe that has lived around Lake Turkana for centuries. Interestingly enough, a Nile perch of Turkana can reach the enormous size of over 300 pounds.

When the sun went down back at the camp, the sky blazed crimson over the lake. A strong wind immediately began to howl from across the lake like a sandblaster, blowing sand and tiny pebbles everywhere. We had purchased charcoal in Loyangalani and made a cooking fire behind some rocks to escape the full force of the wind. Elaine had cut up large chunks of Nile perch, smothered them in canned butter and garlic, and then wrapped the fish chunks and potatoes in aluminum foil. Who would ever believe that one could dine on gourmet perch beside a lake in the middle of a scorching desert?

It was now our farewell to this safari—for this family of gypsies who had shared everything together. Oh, the wonders we had seen! It was an awkward silence in the wind. Everyone was trying to find their voice, their good-byes—like families of nomads trying to forestall the disbanding of large settlements to go on their separate ways.

"You know, we wish this safari could go on for another month!" Brian and Pete spoke up.

"What do you mean, another month? How about for a year?" Aya and Ulla rejoined. "We truly have been like a close family, and it's going to be hard to say good-bye. We have experienced things other people only *dream* about, and for that, we are grateful."

"Another year, huh?" Jack said. "Knowing all of you so well, I believe you really *do* want to be chased by an elephant again, ride on another *matatu* with Margaret to Homa Bay, dig more sand out of the Chalbi." Then Jack smiled wryly at Elaine. "And take more mud baths in Marsabit."

We agreed that some discomforts made it all real.

But Orange Blossom, this time, was at a loss for words. She got up from the table silently, hurried over to the Land Rover, and soon returned with her tape player. She put in her Johnny Mathis tape as no one spoke. She smiled. We knew the words by heart. The lyrics of "There is someone walking behind you . . . turn around, look at me" were carried off by the strong night winds of Lake Turkana far away into the desert.

I knew my safari pals, especially Orange Blossom, would be walking only one step behind me forever in my memories.

140

# INDEX

**Dick Houston** was born in Ashtabula, Ohio, and educated at Kent State University and Edinboro University of Pennsylvania. At various times during the past twenty years, the author has traversed the African continent on safaris across the Sahara Desert and into the rain forests of Zaire, from the vast East African bush country to the swamps of Botswana's Okavango Delta. He presently teaches writing at the American Embassy School of Lusaka in Zambia. His writings and photography on African subjects have appeared in *Smithsonian*, *Reader's Digest*, *The New York Times*, *Travel-Holiday*, as well as other publications around the world.

On breaks from teaching, he is off on new adventures, either white-water rafting on the Zambesi River, following the last great elephant herds still found in central and southern Africa, or setting up a new campsite deep in the bush under the dome of African stars—far from the madding crowd.